"Who texted y

He could at least get a trace going. But this was Halle's first time back in Blueridge in fifteen years—a fact he'd been grappling with for weeks now. And he doubted she'd kept in touch with anyone here. She hadn't kept in touch with him. Still, he continued with "Did you recognize the number?"

She looked around, then tilted her head back and closed her eyes. "I dropped my phone when you tackled me to the floor."

"Or when I saved your life, but you can thank me later." He was already on his way to the door. "I have to get back downstairs. I want you to stay here, lock the door behind me and—"

The rest of his directive—which Kyle wasn't even certain Halle was going to follow—was lost as a loud blaring sound pierced the air.

Halle jumped, and her gaze landed back on him.

"Fire alarm," he said as a fresh ball of worry filled his gut. "We have to get outta here!"

Lacey Baker, a Maryland native, is a wife, mother, nana and author. Family cookouts, reunion vacations and growing up in church have all encouraged Lacey to write heartwarming and inspirational stories about the endurance of family and finding love. She is the author of Hallmark Channel Original Movies *A Gingerbread Romance* and *Christmas in Evergreen: Bells Are Ringing*, as well as *Snow Place Like Home*, a Bellepoint novel.

Books by Lacey Baker

Love Inspired Suspense

Lethal Reunion

Visit the Author Profile page at LoveInspired.com.

LETHAL REUNION

LACEY BAKER

LOVE INSPIRED SUSPENSE
INSPIRATIONAL ROMANCE

LOVE INSPIRED® SUSPENSE
INSPIRATIONAL ROMANCE

ISBN-13: 978-1-335-63860-1

Lethal Reunion

Copyright © 2025 by Lacey Baker

Recycling programs
for this product may
not exist in your area.

Love Inspired
22 Adelaide St. West, 41st Floor
Toronto, Ontario M5H 4E3, Canada
www.LoveInspired.com

Printed in Lithuania

MIX
Paper | Supporting
responsible forestry
FSC® C021394

And be not conformed to this world:
but be ye transformed by the renewing of your mind,
that ye may prove what is that good, and acceptable,
and perfect, will of God.
—*Romans* 12:2

To Rev. Dante K. Miles.
My pastor and my friend.

ONE

"Lord, give me strength," Halle Jefferson whispered as she walked into the room filled with former classmates who'd graduated with her fifteen years ago.

If coming back to Blueridge was a mistake, it was too late to do anything about it now. She took another step, just to prove she could do something other than contemplate and doubt—which had been her go-tos for the past few weeks. Clasping her purse in front of her, she forced in a breath, holding it a few seconds before releasing it slowly.

A few feet away, two familiar women were clutching hands and giggling just like Halle recalled them doing in high school. They walked right past her as if she wasn't there. Perhaps it was the rather plain black cocktail dress she wore. She'd wondered if she should've gone with a brighter color or done something different with her neat pixie-cut hairstyle. She glanced down at her dour outfit and shrugged. At least her shoes were cute—black pumps with sparkles that made them seem like a star-filled night. They were also new, a splurge she very seldom allowed herself.

It hit her suddenly that her clothes weren't the reason those two women, or anyone else so far, hadn't noticed her. They wouldn't know Halle Jefferson standing alone with a death grip on her purse. Not when they would've always seen Halle and Stella together—"The Twins" as they'd often been called. While they'd never dressed alike, she and Stella were identical twins, born two and a half minutes apart. And they'd done everything together. To be fair, in a town the size of Blueridge, everybody seemed to do everything together.

But Halle and Stella had literally done all the things side by side. From jogging every morning to joining the church and signing up for every music class and any other activity they could find. They enjoyed each other's company, which was a plus, but that wasn't the main reason they stuck so tightly to one another. It was because they were all each other had in this world. Their parents had died in a boating accident when the girls were ten years old, and they'd been shipped here to the slow-paced Western Maryland town of Blueridge to live with their father's bitter and drunken brother.

They'd been best friends in addition to being sisters, so when Halle lost Stella, she'd lost everything.

Fifteen years. That was how long it had been since her sister was found strangled behind the bleachers of their high school football field. And fifteen years that her killer had remained free.

Take a deep breath. That was what her therapist would say as Halle felt her pulse quicken with the memories.

My peace I give unto you. The words to one of her favorite scriptures came next.

Halle let both phrases run on repeat in her mind for what felt like an eternity but was more like a few moments. Another glance around the room and there were more faces she remembered, more names and tidbits about their families that bubbled up.

Enough of the past. Those words were a roar. A command she willed herself to follow. Then she took another step forward and tried to loosen her grip on her purse. She favored small bags and this beaded clutch went perfectly with her shoes. It was also big enough to hold her phone, room key, lipstick and inhaler, which was thankfully all she needed to spend a couple hours at this welcome mixer.

Not too far away was a table with beverages. That table was near an alcove where she could hide out for a while. Once again, she second-guessed coming back to this town. There were too many bad memories here, but she'd also had this feeling that she needed to face those memories or she'd never be able to take the next steps toward the future she'd dreamed of. So she'd accepted the invitation to attend her fifteen-year class reunion and to open the time capsule Stella, their class president, had locked away at the end of their senior year.

Her sister had loved school projects while Halle had despised them. The time capsule had been Stella's final project. Five items that reflected highlights of their senior year had been locked away, to be reopened and reminisced over fifteen years later. Her sister had been thrilled to see it through to the end. Unfortunately, Stella's end had come too soon.

Despite that, the alumni committee had decided to go along with this ceremony as Stella planned. New items would be added, which had already been selected, and all Halle had to do was stand there and smile while she put them into the capsule and then another ordeal in Blueridge would be over.

Forcing herself to move again, Halle started toward the beverage table. She needed a drink and then to sit down for a few minutes to get herself together. The vibration of her phone inside her purse stopped her and she sighed while considering whether to pull it out.

It was probably Stefan, her manager. He'd been calling her every day since he'd announced her international tour. She would play in seventeen venues around the world, a mixture of classical and jazz, her favorite. The tour would start in four weeks, so publicity had already begun. Stefan no doubt wanted to tell her about another interview or a photo shoot to accompany the press releases. Nothing she felt like dealing with right now. But if she didn't answer Stefan's call, he'd simply call her right back. He knew she had no personal life and that the only reasons she wouldn't answer were not being near her phone or being asleep—and really, he didn't often care if the latter was the case. He could be extremely annoying at times, but he was a great manager and she appreciated all he'd done for her over the years.

She had already begun to pull the phone from her purse when she realized it wasn't ringing. The vibration must have been a notification—something she probably could've ignored—but since the phone was in her hand now, she navigated to the text messages.

You look lovely tonight.

Her forehead furrowed as she stood perfectly still and read the message again. It was from "Unknown," which made sense because there was no one in her life who would send her a message like this. She was just about to reply with a "sorry, wrong number" text, when another message popped up. From the same sender.

You don't have a lot of time. Do exactly as I tell you and this will be over soon.

Her fingers trembled now. Not enough to drop the phone or her purse, but enough to alert the rest of her body that something wasn't right. She lifted her head slowly, as if moving too quickly might solicit another message or something worse. Although, what would be worse? She was standing in the middle of a ballroom full of people she'd once known but couldn't wait to get away from. This entire trip was probably the worst decision she'd ever made, but that wasn't the priority at the moment.

You always did take a while to catch on. You never were as smart as Stella.

Her heart thumped so fast in her chest and so loud in her ears it almost drowned out the

DJ's music. With quick movements that caused a slight pain in her neck, Halle turned to her left and then to her right, before looking behind her. There were at least a hundred and fifty people in this room, none of whom she'd spotted on their phone. Surely, she hadn't glimpsed each person in that fast look-around but her entire body trembled as fear raced through her.

Who are you? What do you want?

She typed the message with lightning speed then looked around again. Hoping she would catch someone on their phone. And then what? Was she going to march over to whoever that person was and ask if they were out of their mind? Were they intentionally trying to freak her out? Or was she perhaps just overreacting?

Is this a joke?

She hurriedly typed, sent and looked up once more.

Her fingers clenched the phone as she prayed the answer would be "yes." But who would play such a distasteful joke on her? Nobody knew she was coming except for the alumni committee. And whoever else they told, which, considering this was Blueridge, was most likely every student in their graduating class and their families.

You're wasting time. Walk past Dena Savage and head for the long tables at the back of the room.

No! Her immediate response should be no! Whoever this person was, whatever they were doing, had nothing to do with her. And she was over this welcome party. She didn't need to be here tonight. She could go back upstairs to her room and stay there until tomorrow night's ceremony, then on Sunday morning she would be on her way. She was about to drop her phone into her purse and turn around to leave, when it vibrated again.

Or you can end up begging for your life like Stella did.

Her blood froze as she read those words. Music played around her, and people continued to dance and chat and laugh. But tears stung her eyes, fear laced down her spine and she swallowed to keep from screaming.

I see you're ready to listen now. Walk across the room toward Dena.

This was the second time the texter mentioned Stella. And that shouldn't have been much of a surprise since she was back in Blueridge, and she and her twin had always been recognized as a package deal. But…why? She wanted to shout that question while she stood in the middle of this room. The same way she'd shouted when Sheriff Briscoe had come to their house the day after graduation. The tall, burly man had looked Uncle Pete right in the face and said, "Stella's dead." And Halle had screamed. She'd screamed and cried for what felt like the next week, and then she'd stood at her sister's grave and cried some more.

Gulping, she struggled for calm as she glanced to her left to see a woman with her hair in long braids, her smile bright as she greeted someone else. It was the laugh that Halle remembered, the high-pitched giggle that always sounded like a cartoon character instead of the soft-spoken chemistry genius named *Dena Savage*.

Whoever was texting her was in this room. She felt sick and wanted to turn and run. But she glanced at the phone's screen again, reread the words *Or you can end up begging for your life like Stella did*, and gasped.

With her hand shaking so much she had to push her clutch under her arm and put both hands on the phone, she finally typed:

What do you want?

I want you to get the key.

What key? And why are you texting me? If you're
here and you want this key, you can get it yourself.

Or I can rip off that belt you're wearing and wrap
it around your pretty little neck so you'll match
your twin once more.

Her eyes closed and she tried to bite back the
fear rising up in her like a torrential storm—
fear coupled with anger that had her shaking her
head. The repeated mentions of Stella, and this
time with reference to her sister being strangled,
sent waves of dread soaring through her body.
Was this really happening? Again?

The phone buzzed and she jumped.

Walk across the room to the table with the clear
box in the center. The key is inside that box. Get
it and wait for further instructions.

Without further contemplation, she took her
next step on wobbly legs. They wanted this key,
that was all. So she would give it to them, and
then she would get out of this town tonight!

She was cutting across the dance floor, weav-
ing in and out of people executing the line dance
moves directed by the lyrics of the song now
playing. Her shoulder bumped someone else's
but she didn't bother to look at the person or

make any apology. Her focus was on making it to that table. As she drew closer to where the DJ was set up, the music grew louder. So many people were in this room, she couldn't take a step without colliding with someone. But she wouldn't stop.

Trying to walk faster, she stumbled and felt a hand on her arm attempting to steady her. Turning, she glanced at the guy who'd undoubtedly kept her from falling flat on her face—further delaying this task she'd been given. She didn't know him, or maybe she did—she didn't stick around long enough to figure it out. On the move again, Halle could see the table now. It was just about five feet away. There was a glass box on a riser, which was covered in a royal blue-and-gold cloth—their class colors.

She held tight to the phone and when she was finally close to the table, another man's voice stopped her from reaching for the box.

"Are you okay, Halle?"

Kyle Briscoe waited a beat for her to respond. Her fear, now magnified as he stared at her close-up, masked the Halle he remembered from years ago. She parted glossed peach-hued lips to respond even as her brow furrowed. But the sound of glass shattering silenced her and cut through the music.

Noel Crampton, a former classmate who'd run in Kyle's very limited circle, had just stepped between Kyle and Halle, undoubtedly getting ready to speak to Kyle. But then Noel gasped and arched back before falling to the floor.

"Get down!" Kyle yelled as he lunged forward, covering Halle's body with his own as they both went down as well.

Screams joined the music as someone in the crowd yelled, "Shooter!"

Noel was lying on the floor, blood dripping from his shoulder. A couple guys came running over to apply pressure to his wound. Exactly what Kyle would've done before Halle moved beneath him, dragging his attention to her again.

"You almost got me killed," she whispered before pushing at him.

"No, but I am gonna get you out of here so that doesn't happen." Easing back until he could stand, but not at his complete height, he grabbed her arm and pulled her up from the floor. "Stay down and run!"

Halle did as he said but with a frown, so he knew she didn't like him telling her what to do. Only a person who'd known her for eight years and who'd been her boyfriend for three of those years would've known, but that wasn't the point right now.

Chaos erupted in the grand ballroom at the

Blueridge Ski Resort. As Blueridge's sheriff, Kyle should've been the one trying to calm the disruption and find the shooter, but at the moment, getting Halle out of here was his priority.

She was the target. As much as he hated the thought, his gut instinct said it was so, and Kyle always listened to his gut. At least he'd learned to in the past ten years.

He ran as fast as he could without dragging Halle behind him or knocking anyone down. But there was a lot of pushing and yelling. The music had changed even though the DJ was long gone. Kyle kicked a chair that had been knocked over out of their way as he made a dash for the door. Once they were in the hallway with half the other guests, Kyle turned them toward the stairs instead of the elevators.

His room was on the floor just above the ballroom and it took them a few minutes to get up there and run to the opposite end of the hall. Halle was out of breath; the hand still holding her purse went to her chest as she glared at him. Certain she wasn't going to run away—most likely because she was still in shock—he released her hand and dug into his pocket for the key. When the door was unlocked, he pushed it open and said, "Get inside."

Once again, she complied, hurrying into the room. He followed, closed the door and then reached for his phone. "Yeah, Brian," he said after pressing a speed dial number. "How close are you to the lodge?"

"Just coming around the bend." Brian Raker was one of three deputies who worked with him at the sheriff's department. "Tanya's mighty upset, since I told her I'd be arriving with you but—"

"I need backup!" Kyle yelled into the phone, cutting off whatever else Brian was going to say about today's drama with his fiancée. "We've got a shooter!"

Halle dug into her purse and retrieved her inhaler.

"Are you serious?" Brian asked.

"Noel was hit in the shoulder," Kyle continued. "Call for the paramedics and get Lonnie and his guys to set up roadblocks."

"Got it, boss! On my way!" Brian replied, his tone markedly more serious now.

Kyle disconnected the call then turned to Halle. "You okay?"

He'd been the sheriff for almost a year now and so far, nobody had been shot in his hometown. Eight years prior to coming home, he'd been an FBI profiler working out of Quantico. He needed to get back downstairs to work the scene. An active shooter could do a lot of damage and disappear without a trace if given the time. Brian would be pulling up in minutes and he'd take care of crowd control and getting people to safety while Kyle made sure Halle was situated.

"Fine," she gasped after taking her second inhale of medication.

It had been years since he'd seen someone using an inhaler. Fifteen years to be exact. Halle had been diagnosed with asthma when she was five years old. By the time he'd met her, when she was three months shy of turning eleven, her inhaler was as much a part of her identity as the naturally talented way she played the piano at church on Sundays.

"You need to sit down? Or can I get you something to drink?" Once he knew she was okay, he could leave. He still had a job to do, even if watching someone get shot barely a foot away from where his ex-girlfriend stood had rattled him. But wasn't keeping Halle safe part of his job, too? What if his instincts were right and the shooter was targeting her? Moments before the shooting, he'd watched her, moving through the crowd as if the people weren't even there. The distressed look on her face was why he'd followed her, not because she'd been dominating his every thought since he'd learned of her impending return a few weeks ago.

There'd been only one shot and if Noel hadn't

crossed in front of her at that exact moment,
Kyle was certain the bullet would've hit its intended mark—Halle. How could he be so sure
she was the target? Because fifteen years ago,
it had been her sister.

The thought had his fingers clenching into
fists. One shot. That was all that had come
through that window. He'd been listening for
more glass shattering as they ran and was almost positive—even amidst all the noise—that
none had come. Because he'd removed the target.

Halle shook her head. "I said I'm fine." Then
she sighed heavily. "No thanks to you. Why'd
you stop me?" She started to pace, snapping the
cap on the inhaler before dropping it into her
purse. "They said they would... I would end
up..." She paused, shaking her head. "I needed
to follow the instructions. That's all. Just follow
the instructions and then I could leave. But then
you stepped in the way and I couldn't. Why?
Why were you even there?"

Through her babbling he sensed a few
things—anger, adrenaline and the one that irritated him the most, fear. He'd known something was wrong the moment he saw her staring
down at her phone. From the corner of the room
where he'd stood—or decided to hide out—he'd
had a clear view of the entryway to the ballroom. He'd watched her standing still, her pecan-

hued skin appearing as soft as he remembered
it. She hadn't smiled, which she'd done often in
the past; instead, her mouth had been drawn,
her gaze pensive.

"Who told you to do something? And what
were they going to do if you didn't comply?" The
events of the past few moments replayed rapidly
through his mind. She'd been heading to a specific spot in the room before he'd intercepted her.
He thought about the table he'd skirted around
to get to her. On top of the royal blue tablecloth
had been three risers—two smaller ones that
held the championship archery and debate club
trophies won during their senior year. The center riser, the taller one, held a glass box with a
key inside.

"Were you going to get the key? The key to
the time capsule you're supposed to open at tomorrow's banquet?" he asked.

She glared at him, her lips drawn into a tight
line, eyes still wide with shock. If it felt weird
to be standing in the same room with her again
after all these years, he couldn't totally process
that feeling now. Too many questions, too many
scenarios, were playing through his mind and he
needed answers. He needed to get what he could
from her and then go back downstairs to figure
out who thought it was a good idea to shoot into
a ballroom in his town.

What he didn't need was Halle's obstinate nature putting a roadblock in front of his efforts and quite possibly endangering her life even more. "Tell me what's going on, Halle," he insisted when she still hadn't replied.

"I don't have to," she muttered.

"I'm the sheriff in this town so, yeah, you kinda do." He hated having to talk to her that way and despised the contemptuous look she tossed at him in response.

Sighing, he dropped his arm to his side. "Look, I know I don't have to tell you how serious this is. Noel's lying down there bleeding. You saw him hit the floor after being shot just like I did. So, tell me what's going on!"

Her eyes grew wider—cinnamon-brown eyes that had haunted his dreams on too many nights to count. "You're telling *me* it's serious? Silly me, I thought the text messages were a joke. A sick prank designed to freak me out the moment I set foot back in this town. But then there were the threats and now, thanks to you, I've been shot at!"

He hated every word she'd just spoken, the implications behind each one sliding through him with red-hot rage that only amplified his irritation that someone in his town had gotten shot on his watch. "Which is why you need to tell me everything, and I need you to do it now," he said through gritted teeth as he tried to hold on to the last shreds of his temper.

"Who texted you?" he asked, thinking he could at least get a trace going. But this was Halle's first time back in Blueridge in fifteen years—a fact he'd been grappling with for weeks now—and he doubted she'd kept in touch with anyone here. She hadn't kept in touch with him. Still, he continued with, "Did you recognize the number?"

She looked around, then tilted her head back and closed her eyes. "I dropped my phone when you tackled me to the floor."

"Or when I saved your life, but you can thank me later." He was already on his way to the door. "I have to get back downstairs. I want you to stay here, lock the door behind me and—"

The rest of his directive—that Kyle wasn't even certain Halle was going to follow—was lost as a loud blaring sound pierced the air.

Halle jumped. She looked around and then her gaze landed back on him.

"Fire alarm," he said as a fresh ball of worry filled his gut. "We have to get outta here!"

TWO

The hallway was crowded with people as the alarm blared through all five floors of the resort. There were fifty rooms and three suites total in the main building, and in mid-January they were all likely to be filled. With a grimace at just how many people might now be in danger, Kyle needed them all to move faster.

He looked back into the room where Halle was still standing and yelled, "Let's go!"

This time, though, he didn't wait for her to respond or adhere to his warning. Instead, he crossed the short distance between them and grasped her arm. He pulled her along behind him as he left the room again. She didn't resist, and kept up as he moved them down the hallway. More screams, followed by doors opening and guests who hadn't been at the reunion running out of their rooms.

"Is this real? Is there a fire?" one man asked.

"Get to the stairwell!" Kyle instructed them.

"Everybody take the stairs all the way down to the first floor and out of the building. Now!"

They moved fast, going down two flights with people running in front of and behind them. Kyle eased his hand from her arm to clasp her fingers now. He didn't release her hand as they continued to move and Halle never asked him to. When they made it down to the first floor of the lodge, swarms of people were moving toward the front doors. And as if his deputy knew he was wondering where he was, Kyle's phone buzzed in his pocket. He pulled it out and pressed it to his ear.

"What's your position?"

"East side of the first floor lobby," Brian replied. "I'm moving people out to the side lawn until we can get a better handle on this."

"What's Lonnie's ETA?"

"Fifteen to twenty minutes," Brian said, disappointment clear in his tone.

But there was nothing either of them could do about that. The ride up the mountain could be tricky on a regular day. It had snowed last night and they were calling for more storms over the next few days, so the winding roads were slippery, in addition to being pitch-dark this late in the evening.

Backup wasn't going to get here in time. Not for Kyle to get Halle to safety and then take care of everyone else. He had to make a choice, one that didn't sit well with him, but that needed to be made, nevertheless.

"Something's going on that I'll explain later," he said. "I need you to run point here for a few minutes while I get Halle to safety. Then I'll be back."

"Halle?" Brian asked. "As in Halle Jefferson?"

There was a knowing tone in his voice. Brian was a few years younger than Kyle and Halle. He'd been just a freshman when they were graduating, but he'd idolized Kyle and had hung around trying to be anywhere Kyle was, so he knew—just like the rest of the town—how in love Kyle had once been with Halle.

"Yeah," he replied with a sigh. "I'll tell you about it when I get back. Get everyone outside then have the resort security team sweep the entire building."

"Got it!" Brian said.

Kyle stuffed his phone back into his pocket. There was probably no fire in the building, but they would check anyway.

"We're going this way," he told Halle, who'd stood by his side while he talked on the phone. Probably not because she wanted to, but more because she didn't know what else to do.

That made two of them. At least, he didn't know what to do about the thoughts that had started rolling through his mind. If somebody

had demanded she do something, threatened her
if she didn't, then shot at her, the situation was
bad. Now it seemed that same person was shifting gears, deciding to set the resort on fire instead of getting whatever it was they wanted
Halle to retrieve. No, that didn't make sense.
The shooter probably just set off the alarm so
they could get away.

"Why? The door's that way," Halle argued,
snapping him out of his thoughts.

"We're going out the back way." Despite his
gut telling him differently, there was a slim
chance that the shooter had actually set the resort on fire to get to her, or perhaps to get her
out into the open to take another shot. If that was
the case, Kyle didn't want her in the crowd with
everyone else. And if the shooter didn't see her
in the crowd, he'd have no reason to harm innocent people.

They bumped into a few more guests then
turned a corner a little too fast and she stumbled. Turning back, and this time wrapping an
arm around her waist to make sure she stayed
upright, their gazes locked. For just a few seconds Kyle felt like he was sixteen again and they
were at the resort for the annual SnowFest. They
weren't allowed in each other's rooms, so in between activities he and Halle would sneak into
the stairwells to be alone.

"I'm okay now," she said, her voice hitching on that last word. "I'm okay. Let's go."

Right. Yeah, they needed to go. Gritting his teeth at the foolish and pointless memories, he gripped her hand again and took off running toward the kitchen. They went straight through without stopping as all the staff had already left. Kicking the door handle ahead of him, the door flew open and they ran through.

The brutally chilly air smacked at his face, but Kyle kept going. They had to get far away. So far that Halle would be safe and he could figure out who was after her. Because he would figure it out, and when he did… Rage hadn't boiled in the pit of his stomach like this in years. He'd forgone counseling to help curb it and instead meditated on the Word the way his mother had taught him. So he knew he had to trust and believe that the Lord was with them, that He'd cover them and keep them. He had to believe that—no matter how dark and ominous the night grew the farther away from the resort they ran.

Whose bright idea was it to wear sparkly four-inch heels? Halle clenched her teeth at the bitter cold air blowing around and the snow that came midcalf with each labored step she took.

The shoes were cute and had made her feel giddy, an emotion she didn't often allow her-

self to experience. Her dress at least was long
sleeved, but the material—like the shoes—was
meant more for fashion than warmth.

Kyle moved slower now that they were outside, his hand still gripping hers tightly as they
navigated the darkness. It was eerie how dark
it seemed just a few moments after they'd left
the resort behind. From the large five-story log-
cabin structure with warm golden light pouring
from just about every window to the pitch-black
night sky dripping with fat flakes of snow. She
shivered and Kyle stopped.

Grumbling, he reached for her waist again and
Halle froze with alarm. "What are you doing?"

"Getting you out of the cold," he replied briskly
before lifting her off her feet.

One of her arms went around his neck, another across his chest to rest on his shoulder as
he cradled her. But this wasn't some romantic
gesture. It wasn't the walk across the threshold
of their new home on the night of their wedding—something she hadn't pictured in years
but came crashing back like the dream had never
left. "I can walk." The protest died on her lips
as he started running again, this time moving
noticeably faster than he had before.

It was obvious he knew where he was going,
even in the dark. She wasn't as surprised by
that as someone else might've been. Someone

who hadn't grown up in Blueridge. Even with that shared advantage, Halle still didn't know where they were.

"We have to find shelter," Kyle said.

"You're the cop," she whispered as she burrowed closer to his chest. "Why're we going in the opposite direction of everyone else? Didn't you call for help?"

"Yeah, I am and I did," he told her and moved between some trees where he stopped—she suspected to catch his breath.

He leaned back against one of the trees, holding her even closer. She couldn't help it, she shivered. And then hated the implications of that reaction. This wasn't what she'd expected when she decided to come back to Blueridge. Her reaction to seeing Kyle again wasn't something she'd allowed herself to consider. It'd been fifteen years after all; they'd both moved on.

"There're cabins back here. New owners took over the resort this fall and they started some renovation work. We just need to get to one of them, preferably one all the way in the back."

Her teeth were chattering now and she could barely feel her toes. If she had more questions about why they were going to the cabins, she swallowed them along with another gust of cold wind. He took off running again, his strong legs cutting through the deep snow like an experienced mountaineer. She couldn't believe this was how tonight had turned out…that someone had actually shot at her and now she was being carried into the night by a handsome sheriff.

Kyle was still good-looking; no amount of fear or life-threatening events would hide that fact. His mocha-brown complexion was highlighted by soulful russet-brown eyes. He'd grown a full beard and his wavy black hair was an inch or so longer than the close-cropped style he'd worn as a teen. It was obvious that he was a man now—the tall, lanky teenage boy she'd clumsily fallen for was long gone. Just like her sister and all the other happy memories in her life.

She coughed as regret and grief clogged her throat and glanced over Kyle's shoulder to see the lights from the resort fading into the background. But smoke filled the air and she choked on it again. "The resort's really on fire," she murmured.

This was really happening. A bullet had actually whizzed by her, striking a guy before she'd had a second to tell if she recognized him. Somebody had actually taken a shot at her because she hadn't grabbed that key. She wanted to be angry with Kyle, to rage that he'd almost gotten her killed—as she'd begun to do back at the resort—but those words wouldn't come. Mostly because she couldn't stop coughing now, but also because she knew it didn't make sense. Kyle wasn't trying to hurt her, but whoever had pulled the trigger was.

The question was why? She hadn't been here in years and she had no enemies. She could say that honestly, because she had no friends, either. Before she could manage another dismal thought, the world shifted once more as Kyle wobbled a moment and they both fell to the snowy ground. They'd just come to a hill and now they were tumbling down it. Kyle still held her close, both of them grunting during the journey. When they finally came to a stop at the bottom, he stood and scooped her into his arms again.

There was no time for chatting as he moved even faster. His heart thumped against the side of her face, which was now buried against the wet front of his shirt. The wind made an eerie crying sound that was met with the hooting of an owl. Another few minutes that seemed like hours passed as they traveled and she shivered, until finally, they came to a stop.

"This'll have to do," he grumbled more to himself than to her.

It was fine—her teeth were chattering too loud to talk.

He stomped up the steps to the cabin, and it sounded like Kyle was wearing boots as opposed to the very wrong dressy shoes that now felt frozen to her feet.

Setting her down on those partially numb feet, Kyle backed her up until she was against the wall, and he probably felt sure she wasn't going to fall to the ground from exhaustion. He moved a couple steps to the side and began working on the door. It was open in less time than it took for her to once again recall how horribly wrong this night had gone.

"Here, let's get inside." His hands were on her once again and she reminded herself that it was just because she was moving much slower than he was.

Since he didn't appear to be shivering, she assumed her dress was thinner than the pants and shirt he wore. The inside of the cabin was dark and smelled stale. It was also only a fraction warmer than outside, but Kyle closed the door against the elements seconds after stepping in behind her.

Halle didn't move. She couldn't see where to go and figured staying still was the smartest thing to do. More thumping told her Kyle was on the move again. His footsteps mingled with a grunt as he bumped into something. Moments later there was a light and she turned to see he'd pulled out his cell phone and switched on the flashlight app. There was more rustling in the distance and then more light.

Kyle had turned on a burner on the stove. She walked into the kitchen and stood behind him, watching one burner after another alight, until all four were burning bright. Then he moved again. He came toward her and put an arm around her shoulders. "Come on over here and warm up."

Halle walked alongside him, anxious for whatever warmth she could get. A nervous giggle bubbled up and she slapped a hand over her mouth.

"Something funny?" he asked.

She shook her head and let her hand slip away from her mouth. "Just a memory," she said. And when he remained silent, she figured he was waiting for her to share, so she turned to face him once more. "Remember that blizzard that knocked out all the power in town for three days? Uncle Pete was probably the only one too cheap to have a generator, so without power we had no heat." She rubbed her hands together, then released them and held them palm out toward the stove. "Our stove was gas so he turned on all the burners and the oven and left the oven door open." She couldn't help it; tears filled her eyes. "Stella yelled how dangerous it was to keep the stove on that way but Uncle Pete just replied, 'It's mighty dangerous to freeze to death, too.'

Then he made us get our sleeping bags and bundle close on the kitchen floor to stay warm."

Through the dull illumination, she glanced up at Kyle and saw that the corner of his mouth had tilted in a smile. "Your uncle wasn't the only one who didn't have a generator at that time. My mama did the same thing—that's how I knew to come back here and turn this old stove on."

For a moment they just stood there staring at each other, both of them recalling that storm, those memories of a time so long ago. When they were both children, both different.

"I'm gonna go in the back and see if there's something you can put on. Your clothes are soaked. That wasn't intentional," he said, the apologetic tone of his voice surprising her.

"I'm presuming running from a killer wasn't what either of us intended for tonight." She shrugged. "Besides, you got us to safety. Thanks."

His brow rose and he opened his mouth like he planned to say something else, but then thought better of it and clamped his lips shut. He stepped away before she could speak again.

Halle moved closer to the stove. Unclenching her fingers, she startled as her purse fell to the floor. She'd forgotten she was still holding it. Bending down, she retrieved it, this time tucking it under her arm as she stood again. She opened her palms and held them a safe distance away from the flames. He was right; her dress was drenched, her arms and legs freezing and her toes almost nonexistent. Inching just a little closer to the glorious heat, she closed her eyes and tried to focus on getting her body temperature back to normal.

Too many other things were running through her mind, fear circling around each one. She took steadying breaths, reminding herself that she was safe…for now, and that the Lord would protect her. Kyle was proof of that, wasn't he?

She'd be lying if she said she hadn't thought about him at all when deciding whether to return to Blueridge. He'd been such a huge part of her life here and an even bigger part of why she'd had to get as far away from this place and all its memories as possible. Leaving him, letting go of the love she'd thought was the best thing in her life, had been hard. But losing her sister and best friend had been even harder. Halle hadn't known how she'd survive either loss, but she had. Only to circle back to this place and a new threat. She gasped at the fresh punch of pain brought on by that thought.

"Here," Kyle said and she startled again as he wrapped a heavy comforter around her shoulders. "It's a little musty."

That was a lie. It was *a lot* musty, and her nose

immediately crinkled at the sour damp scent. "Thanks," she whispered again.

"I have to go back," he said and stepped away from her.

She huddled deeper in the combined warmth of the blanket and the fire.

Their gazes met and he said, "I'm gonna leave you this." He knelt and pulled up his right pant leg. When he stood again, he reached inside the comforter she'd folded tightly around herself and found her hand. There was a clicking sound and then he pushed the gun into her palm, easing her fingers around it. "Somebody other than me comes through that door, you shoot. Understand?"

Understanding and agreeing were two totally different things, and while her mind battled over which one she was going to do, he released her and stepped back once more. Halle was no stranger to guns. Uncle Pete had kept a few in the house and when she and Stella were sixteen, he'd taught them both how to use them. It was the only thing their uncle had ever taught them.

"I have to go take charge of the scene. It's gonna take the other backup a while to get here." He reached into his pocket for his phone and looked down at the screen. "There's no reception this far back into the woods, so I can't even check on their ETA. I need to make sure everyone else is okay. It's my job."

A job he obviously cared a lot about. "You took over your father's job," she said while the full impact of that reality settled over her. Kyle and his father had never gotten along. Mostly because his father was present for everyone else in town, but absent for him and his mother. Heath Briscoe had been embarrassed by his son's reckless and oftentimes illegal antics.

The look he gave her said he knew exactly what she was thinking. "Yeah," was his curt reply. "Stay back here near the heat. I don't think the light from the stove will be noticeable from the front of the cabin, but I'll check once I'm out there. If it is, you may have to turn it down to one burner. But you've got the blanket. I'll try to find something from the resort for you to change into and bring it back."

What if the shooter was able to find this place anyway? What if she was faced with having to shoot someone? Could she do it? Her heart thumped wildly in her chest as she squared her shoulders and nodded. "I'll be fine."

It wasn't the first time she'd said those words, nor would it be the last time she leaned on the Lord's Word to make them true.

Kyle's response was a nod before he walked away. She heard the door open and close but didn't have a clear visual of him leaving since the dim light from the stove didn't stretch that far. After a few moments, she figured he was on his way and she was alone. Again.

Only this time, she wasn't in a high-rise apartment with locked front doors and a security guard at the front desk. And now, somebody out there was trying to kill her.

THREE

Kyle set out into the darkness still clad in his damp clothes. And he didn't have his gun. He'd been attending the welcome mixer, which the alumni committee had planned as the kickoff to a week of events celebrating their graduating class, as a civilian. Brian and Lonnie were working tonight, which was the only reason Brian had been on his way to the resort. Whenever there was a big event up on the mountain, they made sure law enforcement was there just in case.

Well, tonight's just in case meant sounding an alarm Kyle never thought he'd have to in his small hometown.

He turned back to see if he could tell someone was inside the cabin. He couldn't. No light from the stove was visible through the front windows. This was one of the resort's larger cabins, and it was the farthest from the resort for added privacy. He prayed that would work to his advantage now.

Going around to the back of the cabin, he grabbed a branch from one of the trees, dragging it behind him so the pine needles would wipe away his footprints. With his phone on flashlight mode, he traveled along the same steps he and Halle had taken to get here, trying to eliminate any trail back to her. Snow was steadily falling so his actions might be unnecessary since a fresh blanket of white would start to cover any deep tracks on the ground. Still, he couldn't be too careful.

His phone still hadn't found a signal but the minute it did, Kyle knew exactly who he planned to call. Just as he was certain Halle would never forget finding out what happened to her sister, Kyle had his own memories of Stella's death. Truth be told, that day had shredded the very fabric of their close-knit town. And it had broken the woman he'd loved. More than his own betrayal ever could.

Call it guilt or curiosity—and he'd lay claim to both—but Kyle had never stopped trying to find out what happened that long-ago night. After serving in the army, and against his father's wishes once more, he'd applied to the FBI. Sure, it was still following his father into law enforcement, but Heath Briscoe hadn't seen it that way. Heath's life and loyalty were to Blueridge. The rigid old man had sworn Kyle's allegiance should be the same. But Kyle had other plans that garnered him an arsenal of specialized experience and world travels that he never would've received if he'd done what his father expected of him.

Still, even with his desire to make his own life and live on his own terms, the minute he'd gotten settled into the FBI, he'd started his investigation into the night that had irrevocably changed Halle's life. He'd kept it under wraps for a while, but then when he'd joined a specialized team of profilers that eventually became like family, he'd shared his thoughts with them. Tonight, with Halle back in his life—or rather back in Blueridge—and someone obviously gunning for her, he needed his former team more than ever.

As he approached the resort, a crowd of people still stood outside. Smoke billowed through two windows on the side of the building that housed the laundry room.

"Oh, my stars, Kyle! Did you see what happened?" Janet Trembley, who'd sat behind him in English and chemistry class, and was now very pregnant with her second child, grabbed his arm. "Dan said somebody was shooting and now there's a fire."

Janet's eyes were wide as saucers, her voice just a hint away from hysterical. Kyle placed his hands on her shoulders. "Why don't you come over here and sit down," he said as gently as he could, considering they had to move around a few people and take it slow because Janet was wearing boots. They were the dressy kind with a slippery bottom.

He led her to a trio of benches in front of the hedge that surrounded the resort's main building. There was only one break in the bushes, where steps led to the double glass doors of the entrance. They'd switched the multicolored blinking lights that had been wrapped around the bushes for Christmas to bright white twinkle lights. He brushed snow off the seat of the bench and eased Janet down.

"Where's Dan?" he asked because Janet's bus-driver husband should've known better than to leave his pregnant wife alone at a time like this.

"He went over there to find Brian and ask him what's going on. It's mighty cold out here and we'd just like to get home," she said.

Kyle nodded. "I know. We're trying to make sure it's safe first. And we might need to get statements." Even though, if he couldn't move them back into the resort to get those statements, he was gonna have to tell them all to come down to the station tomorrow.

A woman dressed in the resort's red, black and white uniform approached. She had an armful of folded blankets and he eagerly accepted one before placing it around Janet's shoulders. It occurred to him that, not too long ago, he'd done the same for Halle back at the cabin.

"That's okay. I'm good," he told the staffer when she attempted to give him another one. "Janet, I want you to stay here. I'll find Dan and send him over to get you. He can have you wait in your car."

That would only be marginally warmer but she could at least recline the seat and get a little more comfortable.

In his search for Dan, he bumped into two of the resort's security personnel.

"We got everybody out, Sheriff," the taller, slimmer one named Geoff—as evidenced by the name scrawled on his black jacket—said. "Louis Crandel and his buddies were having a bachelor party in one of the suites and balked about having to leave, but we finally got them out."

Louis Crandel had just graduated from the University of Maryland Eastern Shore. Along with his general studies degree, Louis had returned to Blueridge with a local beauty queen fiancée named Makayla. His mama, Linda Jean, was ecstatic but his daddy, Vernon, who used to play pool with Kyle's father, was still fussing over having to foot the bill for the lavish wedding.

"Louis can be a handful," he said. "Tell me about the fire."

"Started in the laundry room. Looks like two bins full of sheets probably doused with some type of accelerant, match tossed on it and *bam*, fire! There was a box of matches by the door but we left it there for the fire department to look at when they get here. The ceiling sprinklers had turned on by the time we got down there so we went through the space making sure there were no places where anything could be reignited and possibly spread beyond the room."

"You said it was started in a couple of laundry bins?" Kyle asked and rubbed a finger over his bearded chin.

"Uh-huh, probably," Geoff replied. "I mean, I'm not a fire investigator or anything like that, but I know what I saw."

Kyle nodded. "Where were the bins? Near the door or—"

"No, they were all pushed to the back of the room, past the washing machines and dryers. There were three bins right up against that wall, all of them stuffed with I guess sheets and table linens."

He frowned. "Are there windows on that wall?"

Now it was Geoff's turn to nod. "Sure are."

"Right around there, that's where the laundry

room is located?" he asked as he pointed to the other side of the building.

"Yep," Geoff replied.

"Directly below the ballroom," Kyle said, more to himself than to Geoff.

His train of thought was interrupted by the sound of sirens. They weren't too far. Probably at the bottom of the road that led up the side of the mountain to the resort.

"The pros are here now," Geoff said and ran a hand down the back of his head. "I mean the fire pros," he continued after catching Kyle's gaze.

Kyle gave a half smile. "I knew what you meant."

"Hey, boss," Brian said as he walked up to Kyle. "Cavalry's here."

"Yeah, I know," Kyle said. "Listen, first priority is to get the paramedics to Noel."

"Copy that," Brian replied. "It's a shoulder wound, through and through. We've got him lying in the bed of Cooper Grandy's truck over there."

"Good. You get anything from him?"

Brian shook his head. "Just that he was going over to speak to Halle Jefferson since nobody's seen her in years. Told me he'd had a flashback and thought it was Stella. You know he had that crush on her."

A lot of guys had a crush on Stella when they

were in high school. On Halle, too, he suspected, but none of them would ever have admitted that since Kyle had made it clear Halle was his girl from the moment they'd decided to take their relationship beyond the friend zone.

"I want to talk to everyone who was in the ballroom," Kyle continued. "And I'd like to do it tonight before they go home and forget something or have a conversation with someone else that might change what they recall."

Blueridge had an approximate population of fifty-two hundred citizens. The majority of them lived in town, with others spread out on farmland and around the base of the mountain. But word still traveled as if they were a group of twenty all living in the same house. And once the chatter began, details were bound to be added or deleted from the stories.

"We'll let the firemen go in first, see if we can get clearance to go into the building. The ballroom and the laundry rooms will be roped off crime scenes, but if there's other meeting spaces where we can conduct interviews, that would be ideal. I don't want to keep them out here in the cold longer than necessary," he told Brian.

Then he turned back to Geoff. "We'll need a complete list of all the guests checked into the resort. Even the ones staying in the east building over there."

"We evacuated them, too, just in case," Brian told him.

"Good call," he said. Brian was a really good deputy and, as Kyle knew, the younger man was aiming to become sheriff one day. He figured there was no better successor. "Send me a copy of the guest list when you have it," Kyle told Geoff. "And get your men to confirm the whereabouts of every guest in the east building this evening. Brian, you and Lonnie will join me with the ballroom guests. And hopefully we can have everyone safe in a warm bed sooner rather than later."

That was the next priority—get the statements and get the guests out of the cold, but as soon as he'd finished speaking, another thought crossed his mind. Kyle turned so that his back was to the main building of the resort once more. To his right was the side of the building where the ballroom, laundry room and kitchen were situated. To the left, if his memory served, were some meeting rooms and a dining room where they served a huge buffet breakfast. Sleeping rooms were all on the upper floors. Turned around like this, the east building was now to his left as well, down a paved pathway. That building was smaller and behind it were the woods.

Earlier, he and Halle had come out of the kitchen and run through the woods toward the cabins, the lines of the ski lifts high above. Those woods directly faced the ballroom. He was walking before the thought had completely formulated.

"Where are you going now?" Brian asked as he fell into step behind Kyle.

"Into the woods," he said. "That shot came through the window in the ballroom. That's on the first floor, so the only way a shot could come from that direction and at that height was if the shooter was in the woods."

Right on his heels now, Brian said, "Sitting up in the trees like a birdwatcher."

"With binoculars and a cell phone," Kyle replied, recalling what Halle said about the text messages.

He hadn't asked her nearly enough questions about those messages. But she'd said she dropped her phone in the ballroom. He'd want to go look for it himself, but after he walked this line of sight.

They trudged through the snow, him using his cell phone's flashlight again, while Brian pulled an actual flashlight from his belt.

"Footprints," he said when they'd left the parking lot about twenty feet behind them.

They both stopped and Brian directed his flashlight ahead of them. "These ones coming out look fresher. New snow has barely had a chance to cover them completely."

Kyle nodded. "He would've had to be situated up there before the mixer began. Waiting for her to arrive so he could contact her."

"He?" Brian asked. "You know who the shooter was? And who's *her*?"

"These footprints are pretty big, like a size eleven or possibly twelve. Boots, no doubt, see the treads?" He flashed his light on the footprints closest to them and then leaned back, directed his light upward as he tilted his head. "Some of the trees out here are hundreds of years old. Branches are sturdy, they could easily hold a man or a woman sniper, but I'm leaning heavily toward a man." He moved his light across the line of trees. "We'll be able to see better in daylight, but I'm guessing right along this row is where he sat and waited. He could see directly across the way, through the parking lot and into the first-floor windows of the resort."

Brian turned around and aimed his flashlight in the direction Kyle had just spoken of. "Directly to the ballroom from here."

Kyle nodded. And he was willing to bet that with binoculars the guy would've been able to see not only the front entrance of the ballroom, so he knew the moment Halle arrived, but also that table she'd been walking toward.

"Change of plans," he said and started moving again. "Send everybody who isn't staying at the resort home. We'll get their statements in the morning."

"You sure? We got a better chance at accuracy tonight," Brian said, but Kyle was already shaking his head.

"I want to go over everything in the ballroom first," he said. "I want to stand in the spot where the shot came through that window. Find her phone, read those messages." He was walking again and thinking out loud even though he knew Brian didn't know exactly what he was referring to.

"I'll come with you," Brian said, trekking behind him once again in the snow. "And I'll tell Lonnie to get whatever statements he can and have all the others come in tomorrow morning."

"Good," Kyle mumbled as he headed toward the resort.

Brian's compromise on the statements was a good idea, and Kyle was relatively sure it was the only good thing that would come out of what they uncovered tonight.

Three hours later, at twenty minutes after midnight, Kyle entered the cabin again. He called out Halle's name, to let her know it was him, and was only partially surprised when he saw her peek tentatively around the doorway that led into the kitchen. He'd wondered if she would listen to him—if she would stay in the cabin and wait until he returned. Halle had always been smart and resourceful. But she also had a stubborn streak, and if the way they'd left things fifteen years ago was any indication, he was the last person she wanted to see tonight, let alone take orders from.

Yet, there she was, looking as pretty as ever. He had a real flashlight now and directed it toward the kitchen. So the cautious look in her eyes caught him first. Then the quick furrow of her brow before she spoke.

"What happened?" she asked. "You to—took so long." Her teeth chattered and he crossed the room quickly to get to her.

Once in the kitchen he pulled the blanket tighter around her. "Did the stove go off?" he asked, frowning now himself as he looked toward the old contraption.

"No," she said, shaking her head. "I turned it off. Stella's warnings about it being dangerous mixed with the possibility of the shooter seeing the light and figuring he'd come inside had me feeling way too jittery. Figured I'd take my chances with freezing."

"I grabbed one of the staff jackets for you to put on," he told her and then sighed when he realized he'd left it in his truck. "I'll go back out and get it."

"No, I can just get it when we leave," she said. "I'm ready to be as far away from this resort and this town as possible."

The part of him that had been relieved she hadn't left, again, did a little jolt, and he paused as he stood in front of her.

"Well," he said, clearing his throat because the last thing he wanted was for her to hear the slight panic in his tone and take it the wrong way. He wasn't just worried about the danger he'd yet to totally clear out there—he really didn't want her to know how affected he'd been by seeing her again. "It's snowing a lot harder than it was when I left. So much that we weren't able to get all those that were here for the mixer down the mountain safely. Those left behind are double bunking in the rooms the resort kept for walk-in reservations."

"Okay." She said the word slowly, her gaze locked on his. "So, we're going back to the resort? I had a room reserved and so did you, right?"

He nodded. "Yes, I'd planned to take the weekend off and get in a little skiing before Monday rolled around. So, I have a room." He cleared his throat again. "But I told them they could use your room for another couple. When I left, they were moving all your things to my room so you can stay in there. And I'll keep watch in the hallway."

"What? Why?" she asked with another shake of her head. "I mean, I don't really want to go back there, so it's fine that you gave up my room, but why would you sleep out in the hallway and give me your room?"

He pushed a hand into the front pocket of his coat. He'd grabbed his coat when he'd gone into his room to make sure his things would be out of the way when hers arrived. That was after he and Brian walked through the ballroom three times, taking all the notes they could before heading outside to help Lonnie with interviews, getting Janet and a few dozen others on the road, then helping to make sure those who remained were situated for the night. When he pulled out the cell phone, her gaze dropped and she reached for it.

"You found my phone?"

Kyle let her take it from his hand. "I did and I read the texts."

Her head snapped up. "But how? It was locked."

He shrugged. *"To Catch a Thief,"* he said. "I was going to try Stella Claire or your birthdate, but I realized a couple of things. One, you wouldn't want that type of daily reminder, and two, you wouldn't be that cliché. So, I focused on something that always made you smile. You loved Cary Grant in that ridiculous role as a thief who should've been caught if those cops were worth anything."

She didn't smile—and he hadn't realized how much he'd wanted her to—but for the briefest moment there'd been a light in her eyes. "I can't believe you guessed my lock code."

"Yeah, carygrant1955. Only someone who knew you well would know the starring actor and year of your favorite movie," he said and waited for her to react. It had taken the breath out of him when he'd paused after typing in the first few letters of her sister's name and decided to try something else. The movie just popped into his head and he'd actually been waiting for the phone to stay locked after he punched it in because it just couldn't be that easy. And yet, it was. Because he did know Halle, had known her even better than he sometimes thought Stella did. And, to what seemed like her astonishment, he hadn't forgotten any of it.

"It is my favorite," she said and closed her fingers around the phone.

They stood for a quiet moment, neither of them knowing how to follow up just yet. Until he took a step back and decided he needed to stay focused as the sheriff and not as the ex-boyfriend who had dreamed about her more times than he was willing to admit.

"When I said you were the target earlier tonight, I was going on a hunch," he said. "I took the few clues I had and figured this was about you and after reading those texts, I confirmed I was right."

She sighed. "No, it's not about me, it's about that key he wanted me to get. I was supposed to get it and wait for further instructions. And I was going to do it and leave this town because there's nothing good for me here. I should've remembered that from before. I shouldn't have come back."

"You had to come back," he said. "And I think whoever was texting you knew that you would. He wanted you to get this key." He pulled the key from his pocket and held it in the palm of his hand. "The key to the time capsule."

"I'm supposed to open it tomorrow at the banquet," she said.

"But he wanted it tonight." He waited, watching her to see if she knew why—if there was a spark of knowledge in her eyes, if not the light he wished was still there as well. But neither appeared.

Instead, she closed her eyes and sucked in a deep breath. He resisted the urge to go to her. It was one of the hardest things he'd ever done.

Halle was always happy, always smiling. Especially when she and Stella were together. They enjoyed each other's company in a way that often made Kyle jealous, even though he knew he shouldn't be. There was never sadness in her eyes when her sister was close and even when it was just him and her, Halle was focused on living in the moment and being happy in every second. That was before Stella's body was found and before he'd told her that he wasn't going to New York with her after graduation as they'd planned. He'd ached to hold her and hug that pain away from her then, just as he did now. But he remained still.

She opened her eyes again, slowly. "I don't know who he is and I don't know what he wants." Her shoulders squared as she met his gaze once more. "And I don't want to go back to the resort. If we can't get down the mountain tonight, I'd rather just stay here."

FOUR

The incredulous look on his face was unnecessary. She knew she sounded off—wanting to stay in a cabin with no furniture and no heat, in the middle of a snowstorm. But what was the alternative? Returning to the resort where someone had quite possibly just taken a shot at her? Uh, that would be a no for her.

It was already after midnight, so perhaps the storm would be over by morning and they could get on the road. The resort would have their own plows to clear the roads, and, as she recalled, a good number of people in town had snowplows on the front of their trucks and would take care of the rest.

"Are you sure about this?" Kyle asked after he'd gone out to his truck and brought in the coat he'd grabbed for her, plus a blanket. "I brought my gym bag in, too. Figured you could use that as a pillow or something. But I'm positive you'd be more comfortable at the resort."

She shook her head and finished spreading out the blanket he'd brought in. While she could've used it to cover herself, she preferred to put it on the floor, which was dusty and probably a little grimy if she could see it better. In response to his question, she sat down on the blanket and tucked her legs under her. She thrust her hands into the pockets of the oversize jacket and tried to put her face down in the wide collar.

"I think I've met my trauma threshold for the night," she replied.

He nodded and joined her on the blanket. "Here, lay back," he said while he pushed that gym bag against the wall and moved over so she'd have space to get comfortable.

"Thanks," she said as she followed his directive and stretched her legs out. "Sheriff."

He remained in a sitting position, but he looked over his shoulder at her. "Why'd you say it like that?"

"Like what?" she asked with a shrug. "Like I can't believe you're wearing the badge you despised when you were a child?"

He gave a wry chuckle. "Yeah, like that."

"Because I can't," she said. "Being the sheriff of Blueridge was the last thing you wanted to do." It was too easy to recall all the times they'd sat on the swings at the park after dinnertime and talked about their future. "I guess things really changed for both of us that day."

"I didn't want to be sheriff," he replied. His tone was a little softer, heavy with something familiar she didn't want to acknowledge.

"Right," she said, blinking rapidly. "You wanted to join the army. Which was weird because you'd never mentioned that when we talked." Her heart started to beat fast and she stuffed her hands deeper into the pockets of that jacket, to keep them warm and also to keep her fingers from trembling. "Sorry, I don't know why I said that."

"Yeah, you do," he replied.

She didn't want to look at him. He was still sitting up and the flashlights were off so she could barely see him anyway, but she kept staring up at the ceiling. If she just kept her mouth shut there was no way he'd be able to see or hear how much the events of their past still haunted her.

"I know why, too," he continued, even though a part of her thought it might be better to stop this conversation. "Because I didn't go to New York with you the way we'd planned."

"You had a right to your own life," she said, hating that each word felt disingenuous.

A long time ago, he'd said he loved her, and she'd loved him fiercely. He had been one of the most important things in her life, second only to Stella. Losing them both in the span of two weeks had been too much for her seventeen-year-old self to handle. But she had handled it and she'd built a new life on her own. The last thing she needed was him—or any unresolved feelings she might have for him—to interfere with that.

"I made promises that I didn't keep." His words shouldn't have startled her. Kyle wasn't one of those guys who couldn't or wouldn't communicate, especially not with her. Which was only another reason why his out-of-the-blue change of life plans had hit her so hard.

"We had plans," he continued. "You and Stella had gotten into Juilliard and were going to study and perfect your craft until your names were in lights all over New York and around the world. And I was going to find a job in NYC, get an apartment, save up until I could afford to put a ring on your finger and make you my wife. Take care of you, support you, love you."

Those last two words settled on her chest like a brick, and she closed her eyes to keep from gasping. A part of her wanted to scream "Why didn't you?" while another part wanted to run out of this cabin, or at least go to another room. Neither option would make her feel any better. She knew that—had known that coming back here and seeing him would rip this wound open all over again.

"But I couldn't breathe, Halle."

She could hear him suck in a breath and release it, as if he had to prove to her and himself that he could now.

"You know how my dad stayed on my back. If he wasn't preaching to me about my responsibilities to God, to this town, to the life I'd been blessed with, he was yelling at me about whatever I'd done wrong that day. My grades weren't great so I hadn't bothered applying to any colleges. I had no idea what type of job I'd get in New York, or what I'd do while you were studying, or eventually performing. Was I really going to just sit on the sidelines while you chased your dream? And how in the world were you going to respect me if I did? What kind of husband was I going to make?" He huffed. "I'd already failed as a son and a friend. I knew Stella was going to meet with Aaron that night even though she'd sworn they were over. And I didn't stop her."

She was blinking furiously again. She'd known he was grappling with a lot of these things back then, and had thought that going to New York, getting out of this town that seemed to have them both in a chokehold, was going to save him. "I didn't stop her, either," she admitted. "After you left our house that night and I'd climbed the stairs exhausted from getting to the school so early that morning, then the long ceremony and the party at Sharlene's, I just wanted to get out of my clothes and fall into bed. She wasn't in our room when I got there but I knew where she was, so I went to sleep. Figured we'd talk about her third breakup with Aaron in the morning. But when I woke up, she wasn't there."

The last words stuck in her throat and the tears fell. She'd cried so much later that day and for the weeks that followed. Cried, screamed, raged. There'd even been moments that she wished whoever had taken Stella away would meet a cruel end as well. And moments when she'd wished she would never have to see Kyle again. Never have to experience the pain and heartache the two people she'd loved most in this world had put her through.

"I kept looking," he said after long moments of silence. "When I joined the FBI, I started a file and tried to use my new skills to piece things together. But I hadn't been back here for years."

"You didn't come home after the army?" she asked and eased a hand out of the jacket pocket to wipe her face.

"For about a week," he said. "Dad thought the army had matured me, trained me and that I should be ready to join him, but I'd already decided on the FBI. So, he was disappointed in me again. I hadn't expected anything less. I'd really come back to visit my mom's grave. Hadn't been there in around five years by that point."

Natalia Briscoe had suffered from leukemia and passed away in the spring of their sophomore year. If Halle was honest with herself, she'd acknowledge that Kyle had started to change right after that.

"Did you like it there? At the FBI, I mean?" She didn't know why it mattered whether he'd finally found his purpose, his peace, but it did.

"I did. A lot," he said. "I was a good agent, a good profiler. I was part of a great team that turned into great friends. Life was as good as it was gonna get for me. Then my dad had a heart attack last year and I came home." He paused then, just stopped and sat there for a few long seconds. "He died the next day. Two weeks later, when I was just getting myself together to start packing up the house, Belle, down at the town council, brought me dinner. She just showed up at the door with a picnic basket in one hand, a jug of lemonade in the other and walked right into my father's house. We ate and she talked. Told me they wanted me to run in the special election they were gonna have for the position of sheriff because Rupert Matlock, the senior deputy at the time, had decided to retire. Seems

Rupert didn't want the job taking a toll on his health the way it had on my dad's."

"And you did it," she said. "You ran for sheriff and you won because the town wanted you here."

"They wanted another Briscoe to replace the one they'd loved and respected," he replied.

"What did you want?"

There was another long silence. "I wanted whatever the Lord had for me. At the time, it seemed like that was it."

The noise woke Halle. A truck's engine, footsteps, the door opening and closing. She jolted up from the floor, heart hammering in her chest. It was cold, a fact she'd succeeded in not thinking about long enough to finally fall asleep. But she was wide-awake now, thanks to the noise and the fear it produced.

Fear that she chastised herself for giving in to. In all the time she'd lived in New York, she hadn't been afraid. Of course, she hadn't been oblivious, either. One of the first things she'd done after settling into the apartment she shared with a roommate—which had been easy to find despite the short notice—was take a self-defense class. She and Olivia, who played the violin and had traveled from Cleveland, had taken the classes together. A year later, she'd taken a refresher course at the gun range but she'd never purchased a gun. Just the knowledge made her feel stronger, more confident. She needed both as she continued with her life, every day telling herself she would live enough for her and for Stella.

But last night she'd been afraid. Of the text messages, of the dark snowy night and of Kyle. Or rather, what she still felt for him.

"Good," he said as he stood in the doorway and stomped snow off his booted feet. "The road's clear, and Brian, my deputy, is out front in his truck. We're gonna drive down slowly, get you into town and settled in before we start talking to the guests who were in the ballroom last night."

She sat up now, rising to her knees and then standing. Her toes had frozen a long time ago and were now probably in the prelude to frostbite as they were painful when she stood. But she didn't groan. Instead, she bent down to grab the edges of the blanket.

"Our classmates," she said with her back to him as she folded the blanket. "Those were our classmates in that ballroom. I recognized a lot of them. But they didn't recognize me."

"I doubt that," he replied and came around to grab the other end of the blanket. They now stood about four feet apart. "I remembered you the minute I saw you."

She tilted her head slightly as she stared at him. Sunlight, in that almost blindingly bright hue that only seemed to appear after a snowstorm, streamed through cream-colored blinds at the window.

"You're biased," she replied.

The corner of his mouth lifted in a half smile that was way too familiar. Kyle had always been a handsome man. The neat beard he now sported and the shorter haircut refined the bad boy she'd been so smitten with. While the broad stretch of his shoulders and the deepening of his voice gave hints of the man he'd become.

He closed the space between them, bringing the four edges of the blanket they were holding together, and his fingers brushed over hers. Her gaze dropped to where their hands touched and remained locked there until another thought burst into her mind.

"The person who texted me knew who I was, too," she said quietly. Then her head snapped up and she found him already staring at her. "They knew who I was, knew I would be there last night and knew my phone number."

"True," he said with a slow nod.

"How would they know all of that? And why would they know? Why would anyone care that I was coming back for the reunion?" she asked and saw the brief flicker of irritation and then anger in his eyes.

He took a step back. "I don't know," he said tightly. "But I'm going to find out. Get your purse. I'll grab my gym bag and we can get going."

"What will happen now that you have the key to the time capsule?" She finished folding the blanket, then squatted again to grab her purse from the floor. Her phone was inside but it was probably dead by now. "Will they come for me again? Try to finish what they failed at last night?"

Without her even realizing it, her chest had started to rise and fall swiftly with heaving breaths. She'd tucked the blanket under one arm and clenched her purse in both hands. "They want that key and I didn't get it for them," she continued. "They... The message said..."

"Stop it!" He pushed the strap of the duffel bag up onto his shoulder and quickly closed the distance between them. His hands were on her shoulders, giving her a gentle shake as he said again, "Stop it right now! You are safe and I plan to make sure that doesn't change."

"But...but..." She tried to get the words out. They were floating around in her mind, a warning flashing in neon lights that she needed to take seriously.

"No buts!" he said through clenched teeth. "I will not let anything happen to you. Nothing, do you hear me? Nothing."

His eyes burned with an intensity she'd never seen before. His brow furrowed and his lips thinned. There was a hole in his left earlobe where he used to wear a gold stud or the gold letter H he'd bought when they'd gone into the city to explore the new outlet mall.

"Do you hear me, Halle?" he asked, snapping her thoughts out of the past.

"Yes," she said and shook her head. "Yes." She swallowed, then sighed.

The fear was back and she hated it.

FIVE

She was sitting in the passenger seat, only the console separating them. Last night she'd slept on one side of the cabin's front room. He'd tried to find a modicum of comfort on the other side. Afraid that if he closed his eyes for too long that something might happen to her, or worse, that she would be gone.

Ultimately, neither had happened but instead of immediately finding sleep, he let memories flood into his mind, let every moment from the first day he'd met her until the day he'd walked away from her, replay like some sappy love movie. Well, not quite. In those sappy love movies, the couple usually ended up together. But in reality, he'd made his way to the bus station and left Blueridge for what he thought would be forever.

He'd missed her every day. Her smile, the sound of her laughter, the way she always hummed with delight when she ate French toast drenched in powdered sugar and maple syrup. The sight of her fingers moving effortlessly over the piano keys. He loved watching her play. Not just hearing the way the notes on the sheet music came to life under her tutelage, but the way she looked when she played. Sometimes she would close her eyes—to feel the music, she'd say. Her body would sway with the melody, or she'd simply tilt her head to one side and breathe in and out, let every note flood the air around her.

"How do you know how to play the piano?" he asked the first time he'd seen her in the sanctuary.

Blueridge had one church with its tall steeple and stained-glass windows. Not everybody in town attended either of the two Sunday services, but he always did. His mother wouldn't have it any other way. Although Heath frequently took the Sunday morning shift at the station, so the deputies could attend services with their families.

She shrugged. Her hair was long then. A perfectly straight part down the center and two midnight-black braids that hung past her shoulders. She was ten, just like him. He knew because he'd heard Mr. Bethel, their Sunday school teacher, say it when he and Ms. Joan were talking downstairs in the fellowship hall.

"My mama used to play," she said, her voice

so soft he'd barely heard her. "She taught me a little."

He didn't really know anything about playing musical instruments. He liked listening to music on the radio or CDs but that was mostly hiphop and some R&B—the dance songs, not those lovey-dovey songs.

"Your mama's dead," he said and pushed his hands into the front pockets of the slacks he wore. He'd forgotten his belt that morning, so the motion pushed the pants a little farther down his hips. But the yellow dress shirt his mother had pressed so crisply it felt like new was long enough that he wouldn't totally embarrass himself or his parents.

She stopped playing and looked up at him. Her eyes instantly watered and for the first time in his life, he'd felt terrible without anyone having to say a word to him. Of course he didn't apologize, but he did hurry to change the subject before any tears fell. If he felt bad now, he knew he would feel worse if he actually made a girl cry—especially this girl.

"Why would somebody want to kill me?"

The sound of adult Halle's voice pulled him out of his reverie and he glanced over to see her staring out the passenger-side window.

"What?" he asked even though he thought he'd heard her question clearly. He just hadn't liked it, especially not coming from her in that slow and steady tone.

She was trying to hold it together. He knew this because he'd watched her do the same in those first few days after Stella's death, when everyone from town poured into Pete Coleman's house. Mr. Pete had fussed and cussed every single day that his house was full of people, but Ms. Annie, the minister of music from the church, and the other ladies from the bereavement ministry ignored him. They fixed so much food and set it out on the dining room and kitchen tables. Everybody who came to pay their respects was urged to sit down and enjoy a plate of food, as if they were being thanked for showing up and saying the obligatory, "Sorry for your loss."

"Why would someone want to kill me?" she asked again.

He could lie to her and say they weren't, but the fact was he definitely thought someone had tried to kill her. "That's what I'm going to find out."

"Do you think this is connected to Stella's death?" was her next question. "I read the texts again this morning and the sender mentioned Stella three times. Like they knew exactly what happened to her."

Which, to Kyle's way of thinking, meant who-

ever had been texting her was a native of Blueridge.

"I don't want you to worry about that right
now," he said while his hands gripped the steering wheel tighter.

They were approaching a part of the road that
was winding and a little tricky to maneuver on
a clear day. This morning, after they'd accumu-
lated two additional feet of snow, it posed even
more of a problem. Especially since the plows
had barely cleared the two lanes going in opposite directions. The shoulder was covered in
foot-high embankments at some intervals, and
the thin layer of snow still packed on the roads
wasn't friendly, either. There were good snow
tires on his town-issued vehicle and Brian's as
well, so they should be okay. Still, he and his
deputy would drive as safely as they could.

"Wanting answers doesn't equate to worrying," she replied. "I just need to know what's
going on. I didn't know the last time and—"

"This is not like the last time," he said, cutting her off. Because this wouldn't be like the
last time, not if he had anything to say about it.
"Once I get back to the station and start talking to witnesses, I'll have a better idea of what's
going on."

"And you'll tell me, right?" she asked and
when he didn't immediately answer she contin-

ued, "I want to know what's happening, Kyle. I want to know when you catch whoever that shooter was. You owe me that much."

There was so much meaning to those last words, but it was time to stop thinking about who he and Halle were in the past. Now he needed—and she needed him—to be the sheriff and get to the bottom of this situation. That was a lot easier said than done, hence his trip down memory lane just a few minutes ago.

"I'm not going to keep anything from you, Halle. I never have." He added that last part because he wanted her to remember something good about him. Since it seemed she was still carrying around old hurts.

"Let's talk about something else," he said, hoping to relieve some of the tension inside the truck. "How are things with your career? Last I heard you were selling out at venues."

"I don't want to talk—"

She never finished the sentence because the first shot took out the right front tire and the truck swerved.

"Get down!" he yelled as he grabbed the steering wheel and tried to keep them from smashing into one of the embankments.

Another shot ripped through the air and then another. If he never heard the sound of shattering glass again Kyle knew it would be too soon.

"Get down!" he yelled to Halle again when he saw she was still upright in the seat, eyes wide and focused on the front windshield.

She moved at the second command, fiddling with the seat belt. But he reached over, placed his hand on top of her head and urged her down in the seat. The seat belt finally gave and she crouched even lower until she was curled into the small space on the floor, her arms folded over her head. Shots were coming faster now, and up ahead Brian's truck swerved, too.

Kyle wanted to keep driving, to get them out of the line of fire as quickly as possible, but the blown-out tire on his truck wasn't going to allow that. He turned off the road the second he saw a break in the embankments. There was still a pile of snow here, but it was substantially lower and he had no other choice. He slammed his foot on the gas and prayed they'd get far enough off the road and into the trees that whoever was shooting at them would no longer have a direct shot. The truck plowed through the snow with a loud boom. Inside they were jolted back and forth and when he glanced down to check on Halle, she still had her head lowered. She was mumbling something but he didn't try to figure out what. When branches crashed into the windshield, he slammed his foot on the brake and they skidded another couple of feet before coming to a jerking stop.

His head barely resisted slamming into the steering wheel and he thanked the Lord there was no impact so the airbag didn't deploy.

With hurried movements he unhooked his seat belt and leaned over the console. His hands were on Halle as soon as he was able to reach her. Moving quickly over her head and down to her arms.

"Are you hurt?" he asked as his heart slammed into his chest. "Did you get hit?"

She was still saying something as she lifted her head and looked up at him.

"I shall fear no evil for—" She snapped her mouth shut, eyes wide with fear.

"I need you to get up so I can check you," he said, trying with all his might to calm his tone. She was afraid and praying, and he could relate to both. "Just… I've got you, baby. C'mon," he continued and tucked his hands under her arms to lift her up.

When she was once again upright on the passenger seat, he moved his hands down her legs to her ankles and back up again. "Thank You," he whispered. "Thank You." She wasn't bleeding; she hadn't been hit. *Thank You, Lord*.

Then, before he could think about whether he should, he pulled her into him and held on. He held on so tightly and continued to whisper his thanks. If she'd been shot… If she died. No, he wasn't going to allow himself to go there. Not today. Not ever.

"I'm okay." The two words were choked out eventually. "I'm okay."

She said it a little louder the second time and Kyle forced himself to loosen his hold.

They both jerked as they heard more gunshots.

"Stay here!" he yelled this time and released her.

He turned to the door, opened it with one hand and grabbed his gun out of the holster with the other. The moment his feet hit the ground, he crouched, extended his arms and aimed his gun straight ahead.

Brian had stopped, too, his truck turned almost completely around in the middle of the road. Right behind it was another black SUV, a more recent model than the sheriff's station ones. The second he saw the woman rise from a stooped position at the front of the vehicle, her arms extended toward the trees, he gave an inward sigh of relief. Then he took off running.

SIX

"He was in the trees, Sheriff," Brian said twenty-five minutes later when they were all at the station. "I heard that first shot and saw you swerve through my rearview mirror. Then the other two shots came and one hit my back window. Next thing I know, we were both swerving. I was trying to get control of my truck, turn around and return fire. Then you came barreling around the side of me, flew right off the road and I 'bout lost my mind 'cause I thought you were hit."

Brian removed the navy-blue skullcap with the Blueridge shield on the front and rubbed the back of his hand over his forehead. He was sitting down behind his desk now.

"Here, you drink this," Shirley said and set an oversize black mug with "fancy work cup" in bold white print onto the desk in front of him. "Calm your nerves."

Shirley Kane was the receptionist at the station when Kyle had gone into the service. She was spry and astute in her early fifties back then. Now, with her salt-and-pepper hair, caramel complexion and signature glossed red lips, she was just as lively and in-charge in her mid-sixties.

"Getting you a cup next, Sheriff," she said with a nod as she passed where Kyle sat on the edge of Lonnie's desk.

"Thanks, Ms. Shirley," he replied. He didn't want a cup of coffee. His stomach was still churning with a dark combo of rage and fear. Adding even a gulp of Ms. Shirley's steaming hot dark roast to that mixture didn't seem like a smart thing to do, but he wasn't about to tell her that.

For what he knew was the billionth time, his gaze landed on Halle. She sat in a chair directly across from him. Ms. Shirley had taken care of her first, flanking her the moment Kyle ushered her into the station. In addition to the piping hot mug of coffee Halle now cupped in both hands, Ms. Shirley had also found her another fleece throw to put over her legs. As one of his deputies usually took the overnight shift, there were several blankets, throws and all sorts of other homey things, including the cot in the back room that Ms. Shirley had brought in for them to use.

Agent Tamera Newberry was leaning against

the wall right next to where Halle was seated. Which was why the moment Kyle lifted his gaze from Halle's solemn face, he met Tamera's amused stare.

"You agents want something else?" Ms. Shirley asked. "Lonnie's on his way in, but I can run down to Della's Bakery and grab some muffins or something. Seems you should put something in your stomach after such an eventful morning."

"No, thank you, ma'am," Tamera replied. "But I do think better introductions are in order now."

Kyle knew that was coming. After he'd gotten back to the road the shooting had stopped. For a few seconds the four of them—Brian, Tamera, him and Najee—stood there and he'd done a rudimentary introduction, in between them all trying to figure out what had just happened. The priority had been getting everybody out of harm's way, just in case their early-morning shooter decided to take aim again. So he'd gone back to his truck to get Halle out. The two of them rode back into town in Brian's truck.

Kyle cleared his throat. "Agents Tamera Newberry and Najee Palmer, you've already met Deputy Brian Raker. And this lovely lady is our wonderful receptionist, Ms. Shirley," he said. "Ms. Shirley, Tamera and Najee were part of the profiler team I was on back in Quantico."

Halle lifted her head. She looked from Kyle

to Najee, who was sitting behind the desk that Kyle sat on, and then back to Kyle again.

"Tamera, Najee," Kyle said, "this is Halle Jefferson. She used to live in Blueridge."

And she used to be the love of my life.

Those words floated effortlessly through his mind and Kyle didn't bother trying to shake them off. He knew he should. Now was the time to focus, not reminisce, but they'd just been shot at. He was giving himself the grace to allow a thought that made him feel good, to attempt to assuage the anger bubbling inside him.

"Hi," Tamera said as she pushed away from the wall and took a step around so that she could stand in front of Halle. "It's nice to meet you, finally. We've heard a lot about you."

"You have?" Halle asked tentatively as she reached out to set the mug on the desk and then accepted Tamera's outstretched hand.

Tamera was a tall woman, with a deceptively slim frame. More than one time he'd seen an unsub take her size and easy tone for weakness, only to be dropped to their knees instantly when they attempted to make a move. She wore her hair in golden-hued braids that normally hung to the middle of her back, except for now, when she was in the field and opted to pull them up into a tight bun at the base of her neck.

"Girl, this man could not stop talking about

you," Tamera continued. "Not even after not seeing you for years."

Kyle could only frown at the extra information Tamera was giving out, while behind him Najee chuckled.

Najee Palmer was a third-generation FBI agent and the smartest computer guru Kyle had ever met. He was only an inch or two shorter than Kyle's five-foot-eleven stature. His bald head all but gleamed beneath the fluorescent ceiling lights and deep dimples showed in his cheeks as he continued to grin when Kyle turned back to glare at him.

"What? She's not lying," Najee said with a shrug. "You did talk about her a lot."

"He also talked about your sister's murder," Tamera added and the room went silent.

Kyle inhaled deeply and waited until Halle shifted her gaze to him. He knew she didn't want to talk about this and had tried to wait as long as he could before he had to take her back through the most painful time of her life. But there was no escaping it now. They had a serious issue on their hands and if they were going to get to the bottom of it, they needed her.

"I called Tamera and Najee last night," he said by way of explanation.

Halle hadn't asked and Brian already knew because he'd told him this morning while Halle had been in the cabin still asleep. "It was the Lord's impeccable timing that brought them up the mountain just as we came under fire," he continued.

Tamera pushed her hands into the back pockets of her jeans and nodded. "He's right. As soon as we came around that corner, we heard the shots, saw your trucks up ahead and pushed it as fast as we could."

"The shooter was in the trees again," Brian said. "Just like last night. The shots came from high up, like he was waiting for us to come down the road."

"He was," Najee said. "Knew there was only one way in and one way out from the resort, so he waited."

"But how did he know we were still up there?" Halle asked. "How do you even know it's a he? I don't understand any of this."

Kyle stood and walked closer to where Halle sat. Tamera stepped to the side, but she didn't move too far away. The other agent knew exactly what Kyle was getting ready to do. They'd done this so many times in the past, worked as a team to solve the most heinous of cases across the nation. And yet, this one murder of a person who had been so integral in his life, had always stumped Kyle. Not again, he told himself. He would not let something else happen in this town, to this woman in particular, without getting to the bottom of it.

"The first thing we do with any case is to look at victimology," he said as he stopped in front of Halle. He squatted so that she didn't have to keep looking up at him.

"I don't know what that means," she said.

He reached for her hand and prayed she would let him hold on to it. A part of him needed to touch her in this moment. He needed to remind her of the connection they once had. Needed her to trust him in the way she once did. He stared down as he took her hand in his, watched his thumb rub along the back of her hand as he held it for just a moment.

"That means we compare all the facts we have about the victims in a case. Last night you were his intended victim," he said. "And we believe it's a *he* because we found footprints in the snow heading into and out of the woods at the resort."

She sucked in a breath and kept her gaze on him. "Okay. What else do you do?" she asked.

There was that resolve again. The squaring of her shoulders and the firmness of her lips meant she was ready to handle business. That whatever emotions she had, she was burying them to get through this, just like she'd done before. Kyle didn't like that look or the stance, but he could still, on some level, respect and admire it.

"Well, in this case, since we believe you're the only target, we look at you and your life and we ask why," he told her. "I asked about your life in New York when we were in the truck."

She nodded. "Right. You did." She cleared her throat. "Okay, I graduated from college, played intermissions for Nicola Colbert for two years until I found my own manager and started to secure my own engagements. I've traveled a bit, played a number of small concerts. That's really all I do is work."

And that admission made him sad. But he continued.

"Any guys? Long-term? Flings?" Tamera asked and Kyle was grateful.

The last thing he wanted to talk about was Halle with another man. As important as the knowing was right now, he hadn't wanted to be the one asking that particular question.

"Nothing long-term," she said and glanced at Tamera. "My focus is my music. I don't have any friends, either. I mean, not the kind that I hang out with or anything like that. I know a lot of musicians from school and from running in the same circles, but nobody I would call an enemy."

"What about musicians that may be jealous of you?" Najee asked. "Maybe you took a job away from someone?"

She shook her head. "Not that I know of. Then

again, my manager, Stefan—his name is Stefan Decater…" She paused, blinked, recalibrated. "He handles all my bookings so he would probably know better if that were a possibility. But I really doubt it."

"The man who texted you last night wanted you to get the key to the time capsule. He knew you were supposed to open it later today but he wanted it last night," Kyle said for the benefit of Tamera and Najee.

"That means he knows you," Brian spoke up. "He had to know you were coming back to Blueridge for the reunion."

"Then why not wait until this evening when I was supposed to open the capsule anyway?" She eased her hand out of Kyle's grip and rubbed two fingers at her temple. "I wondered that. I even told him he could get it himself."

"And how did he respond?" Tamera asked.

"I'll get a copy of the messages printed out," Kyle said.

"He told me I was always slow to respond and that he'd…" Halle paused, swallowed. "He said that he'd wrap my belt around my neck so I would match Stella." Her sister's name was said on a whisper and the fingers at her temple dropped to cover her mouth.

Before he could say something, reach for her again, hug her, swear he would get the person responsible for this, Tamera reached out a hand and rested it on Halle's shoulder.

"Why don't we find somewhere to get you a hot shower, some clean clothes and food," Tamera said. "We've got to find somewhere to stay in this town, too, Najee."

"Already taken care of," Najee added. "Got us two rooms at a place called the Sunny Day B&B."

"Oh, that's a lovely place," Ms. Shirley chimed in. "And it's just down the street here and to the left on Honeysuckle Way. Sunny Clarkson—well, she's Clarkson-Rubbel now—she runs the place now that her parents, Janice and Bill, are getting on in age and since her daddy named the business after her. She keeps nice clean rooms and has the biggest and best buffet breakfast in town every morning except on Sundays. That's the continental breakfast day seeing as she's also the head of the Sunday school over at the church and she has to be there early every Sunday morning."

"I had a room at the resort," Halle said. "I was just going to stay until tomorrow. Came in yesterday morning, took a chance going to the welcome mixer." Her voice trailed off and she closed her eyes, sighed and opened them again. "Planned to go to the banquet tonight and then right back home tomorrow. But you gave my room away, right?"

Kyle nodded. "Yeah, but you also said you didn't want to stay at the resort."

"I don't," she replied. "You're right. So, I guess I need to ask if there are more rooms available at Sunny's."

Nobody, of the three people in that room who knew Halle from long ago, asked why she hadn't considered staying with her uncle in the house she'd grown up in.

"We can take a ride down there and find out," Tamera said.

Halle stood and so did Kyle. "That's a good idea. I'd love a hot shower, but wait, my clothes are still at the resort, right?"

"I can give Fran a call up there to see if they can have somebody drive them down to you right quick," Ms. Shirley said.

"That should already be on their schedule," Kyle added. "I spoke to one of the night shift managers last night and they said they'd have them delivered wherever we requested."

"Cool," Tamera said. "I'll take Halle with me and get settled, and you do your thing here."

She looked directly at Kyle when she said those last words and he knew what she meant. "I will. And, uh, Halle..." He waited for her to turn back and look at him.

"Yes?" she asked, her eyes familiar and yet almost like those of a stranger as he couldn't get a line on what she was feeling at this exact moment.

"I'll come down a little later and we can go over to Town Hall together," he said. "I want you to open that time capsule before tonight's banquet."

If she wanted to ask him why, she didn't. All she did was nod curtly before she turned and followed Tamera out of the station.

He watched her leave. His heart pounding as the door closed with a *thunk* behind her. Years ago he'd been the one walking away. Leaving her to stand on her uncle's porch because he'd said all he could say and she'd endured all she could handle.

"So, let's go through this slower and with more detail this time," Najee said from behind Kyle.

Continuing to stand there wasn't an option. As badly as he wanted to go with Halle, to keep her in his line of sight until all of this was resolved, and maybe longer, he knew he couldn't. At least, not right now. Scrubbing a hand down his face, he turned and saw that Najee had his laptop open. He used a finger to push wire-rimmed glasses up on his nose and then turned his attention to the computer on the desk.

"This the best y'all have up here in the wilderness?" Najee asked, humor—as always—lacing his tone.

"It works just fine for us," Kyle replied. "And Brian's pretty good at figuring out when it doesn't."

"Yeah, just let me know what you need and I'll try to get it," Brian said as he stood up. "We need a murder board, Sheriff?"

Kyle nodded. "You can bring it out although I don't plan on having any corpse pictures up there this time around."

"You don't think you should add Stella Jefferson's name to the top of our victimology list?" Najee asked.

"Why would this be connected to that old case?" Brian asked. He'd pulled the large white board beside the chalkboard stand so they were both positioned along the side wall of the station. "I mean, we're not thinking that killer's just been waiting around town all these years, hoping that Halle would come back and he could kill her like he did Stella."

Kyle dropped into his chair and propped his elbows up on his desk. Then he stared at the empty board. "Stella was the class president. She was captain of the cheer squad, was on the debate team for three years and sang like CeCe Winans just about every Sunday in the church choir. She was smart and friendly," he said.

"She was the prettiest girl in the senior class," Brian added and shrugged when he caught Kyle's gaze. "You think I'm gonna say Halle was the finest with you sitting there and that big gun holstered to your waist?"

Najee chuckled again and this time Ms. Shirley joined him.

"You're the smart one, Brian," Ms. Shirley said.

"Okay, so she was the 'it' girl," Najee added. "And you should be writing this on the board, Mr. Smart One." Najee's fingers flew over the keyboard of his laptop. "Stella Jefferson was strangled with what was suspected to be a leather belt. Although the murder weapon was never found. A number of witnesses stated she left a party on Jericho Lane at ten forty-five the evening of June seventh. That's what the official report says."

"Sharlene's party. The McFadden family has a farm way at the end of Jericho Road. Around four hundred or so acres, so her mama had all the tents, tables and chairs in town brought out there and set up. There were royal blue and yellow balloons everywhere, as those were our class colors. And so much food, I didn't think I'd eat for a week by the time I finished."

"You were there with Halle?" Najee asked.

Kyle rubbed a hand over his bearded jaw. "I

was. We left around quarter after ten. Halle was sleepy. She was always early to bed and early to rise. While Stella could party all night long." The memory had a ghost of a smile appearing on his face. There were so many ways the sisters were different, but he knew the majority of people only recalled that they were identical in appearance.

"Was it normal for you guys to leave Stella? Did she have a date for the party?" Najee continued.

Brian had grabbed a marker and started a bulleted list.

Kyle sat back in his chair since it seemed he was the witness in this scenario instead of the lead agent. He'd often taken that position with his former team whenever their supervisor, Jeremy Sisco, wasn't around.

He nodded, focusing his mind on that night again. "Yeah, it was fine. We did it all the time, especially after Friday Night Bowl. Three games were about as much as Halle could stand since she didn't bowl as well as Stella or anyone else in our little young adult league. But she always went by way of encouraging other teens from the church to join us. Halle was more into the music and youth and young adult ministries than Stella was."

"But Stella went to the party with the two of you?" Najee asked.

"We all went together. There were about seven of us who left the field after taking a bazillion pictures for our parents and then with other classmates once the ceremony was over. We piled into two vehicles, my old Camry and Derrick Chalmers's Jeep. But before we left, Halle wanted to find Stella to let her know we were leaving. I waited around the front of the house for Halle. Stella came out of the house with Kim Francis and Tasha Mosbey." He would never forget a moment of that night, not as long as he lived. "I told Stella we were about to leave and she said fine. Said that Aaron wanted to talk again but she was only giving him ten minutes, then she, Kim and Tasha were going down to the ice cream shop. Sharlene's mama made half a dozen pound cakes but didn't have any ice cream."

"Were they questioned?" Najee asked. "Kim, Tasha and Aaron?"

Kyle nodded. "Yep. Both Kim and Tasha said that Stella went off and spoke to Aaron, then she went to the ice cream shop with Kim and Tasha just like she planned. That's the last time anybody saw her."

"And Halle left town after the funeral?" Najee asked.

"That poor girl cried and cried. I ain't never seen nobody so sad in my life," Ms. Shirley said.

Kyle agreed. "Stella's funeral was a week and a half later. Halle left three days after the funeral." The day after Kyle headed to the bus stop with guilt draped over him like a heavy overcoat.

"And this is the first time she's been back in town," Najee continued. Not a question this time. Kyle knew the tone, so he waited and let Najee's mind work. "The sister. The one who got away. Did he wait for her all these years? Some killers remain dormant for years and years before something triggers them to kill again. Some like anniversaries, want to relive that first kill with someone familiar. In a familiar place. Make a point."

"The fifteen-year class reunion would make a point," Brian said. "A big one, I suppose."

"So, the sister is back in town. Not just the sister, but the twin." Najee leaned back in his chair now, similar to the way Kyle was sitting. But he lifted both hands, clasped them at the top of his head. "And she's supposed to open this time capsule. The time capsule the sister he killed closed. That's an anniversary. It's familiar. It makes a point."

"But what's the point?" Brian asked.

Kyle sat forward. "Right. What's the point?" He asked the question more of himself than the others. "What was the point in asking Halle to get the key to open the time capsule and minutes later, shoot at her?"

"That part confused me, too," Brian said. "I called the hospital before coming out to the resort this morning and they said Noel was doing fine. He'd probably get released later today."

Najee watched Brian write on the board. "This Noel Crampton, he's the one who got in the way of the shot?" Najee asked.

Kyle nodded, slower this time, as he ran the events of last night through his mind again. "I walked up to her because she looked like she was about to scream in fear or pass out. I asked her if she was okay and she looked irritated to see me. Not shocked but irritated, which I didn't immediately relate to something…uh, something other than our past. But then Noel was there. He yelled, 'Hey, Halle!' and then *bam*! He was going down and I was pushing Halle—" Kyle shot up out of his chair. His fists balled at his sides and he scowled when realization slammed into his gut like a sledgehammer. "He wouldn't have waited all these years to get Halle back here and have her bring him that key, then kill her before those plans could be completed. But he would try to take out whoever got in the way of his plan."

Najee nodded again. "You got in his way last night and this morning," he said.

And he would continue getting in his way, Kyle thought as he grabbed his jacket off the back of his chair and headed for the door. He would continue to stand between Halle and anyone who meant her harm, no matter what the consequence.

SEVEN

Tamera Newberry was an exceptionally pretty woman. With her tawny brown skin, hypnotic hazel/green eyes and even that splash of dark brown freckles over the bridge of her nose, she was gorgeous. Not to mention being a confident, stay-outta-my-way FBI agent. She was the complete package—a woman who would be perfect for Kyle.

A woman who could meet him on his level and relate to all the things that were important to him. Something Halle had obviously not been able to do. Never mind the fact that she'd been a seventeen-year-old girl—grieving the loss of her sister—at the time. To be honest, she had absolutely nothing to offer Kyle back then. Nothing but her bruised and battered heart. And for a while, he'd acted as if that meant the world to him. She'd believed that the two of them had filled gaps inside each other that nobody else ever would. That they each possessed the pieces to the broken puzzle the other had become. They were soul mates and meant to be. Those were all the things her romantic teenage mind had wanted to believe.

And none of them turned out to be true.

"Why, Halle Jefferson, aren't you a sight for these sore old eyes." Halle bolstered a smile as she watched the tall older man come from behind the counter. Before she could utter a word, his long, gangly arms were wrapped around her and pulling her into a tight hug.

It wasn't a bad hug, but hugging hadn't been a big part of Halle's life while she lived in the city. So it threw her off a little and she hesitated before wrapping her arms around him and attempting to return the squeeze.

"It's nice to see you, too, Mr. James." She remembered him. His rheumy eyes and the way he always twirled that toothpick between his teeth like it was flavored with something other than wood.

"Oh my goodness." He pushed back until she was an arm's length away from him. "Still pretty as a picture," he continued. "But you must've forgotten how winter in Blueridge feels. Where're your boots?"

"Oh, um, I think they're on the way. Someone's supposed to bring my bags down from the resort," she told him.

"All right, then I guess that makes sense," he said. "I heard there was some trouble up there last night. Glad to see you're safe, though."

"Yes, sir. I'm safe," she said, wondering how long that would be true. "Um, do you happen to have another available room?"

Mr. James carried himself back behind the counter. "Let me take a look," he said.

She used that moment to glance around the place. It hadn't been too often that she or Stella would come into the B&B. Their summer jobs were at the resort working all the events that took place up there. They were either supervising coat check, or helping with setup and breakdown. It was okay money, but what they'd really enjoyed was having full access to all the resort's perks. The pool in the summer, of course. And because they were employees—even if seasonal—they were allowed to grab free equipment and go up and down the slopes as they pleased during the winter.

"Nice place," Tamera said.

They hadn't spoken during the six-minute ride over here. Halle had been thinking about what happened on the road this morning and this man that apparently wanted to kill her. If she'd been coming up with reasons to dislike Tamera as well, that would forever be her secret.

"Yeah, it is," she replied. "I recall the Clarksons, the owners, being a good family. Sunny was the youngest and there were four boys. One of them, Omar, I think that was his name, he played on the basketball team with Kyle. I don't remember this place being so beautiful, though."

The dark wood paneled walls should've been too much, too retro-looking, but somehow, they managed to seem warm and cozy. Plush hunter green rugs were scattered over the planked floors. Tasteful burgundy-and-green paisley drapes hung at the wide windows that faced the street and a small parking lot along the side of the building. Short, wide candles lined the mantel in the reception area and filled the space with a vanilla scent.

"You spend a lot of time here when you were young?" Tamera asked.

Halle shook her head. "No. I mostly saw the family at the church, or the kids at school. But we walked past here on our way to school every day so I've always known the place. They used to put a life-size Mr. and Mrs. Claus right out on the front porch the first day of December. The second year we lived here, Stella and I came right up to them and introduced ourselves and then told Santa what we wanted for Christmas." She grinned at the memory. "Topper Norris and his cousin Frankie called us silly babies and laughed as they ran off to tell every other kid in our Sunday school class what we'd done."

"I hope you and your sister ran them over with your bikes the first chance you got," Tamera replied.

"Worse," Halle said with a slow smile. "Stella mistakenly spilled syrup in their laps as we helped Ms. Joan serve breakfast before the Christmas pageant rehearsal. They couldn't get it all off and were still sticky when I made a mistake and dropped the bowl of glitter we were sprinkling on the ornaments we were making for the tree. So they had multicolored glitter stuck to the front of their pants. Then *they* were the laughingstock of our Sunday school class."

Tamera laughed and before she could stop herself, Halle joined her.

"Good for you two!" Tamera said and lifted a hand toward Halle.

She didn't hesitate. Instead, she returned the high five and figured she might stop her crusade to hate the pretty FBI agent, since she could obviously see the humor in well-placed maple syrup and glitter.

"I've got another room for ya, Halle," Mr. James said, causing her and Tamera to turn their attention back to the front desk.

"Oh, that's great," she said and walked back to the counter. "I don't have my big purse with my wallet and credit cards with me, but as soon as my bags are delivered, I'll take care of the bill."

Mr. James shook his head. "You don't worry a bit about that," he said. "You're one of us. We know you'll take care of things. Sunny's down in the kitchen still cooking breakfast. It's served until eleven-thirty, right down that hall and to your left. Once you two get settled, you should come on down and fill yourselves up."

"That's a great idea," Tamera said. "All of a sudden I've got a taste for pancakes and maple syrup."

When Halle glanced over at her, they both burst into laughter again. So the next twenty minutes, which they spent sitting in the reception area waiting for her bags to be delivered, didn't go as roughly as they could have since the proverbial ice had been broken. If circumstances were different and if she was inclined to cultivate friendships, and also, if they lived closer to one another, she and Tamera could have been friends. But as it stood, they weren't friends. Tamera was an FBI agent here to investigate whatever was going on. And Halle was a victim. At least that was what Kyle had said. After all these years, it was her turn to be a victim and she was determined to do whatever she could to keep from sharing her sister's fate.

The shower was hot, water pressure excellent, so Halle hated to turn off the water and step into the chilly bathroom air. Her room was just as lovely as the reception area. With plush beige carpet, except for here in the bathroom where the black-and-white-checkered tile reminded her of Uncle Pete's house.

So much about this place brought flashbacks of her childhood. This was a Victorian-style house, just like the one she and Stella had lived in with Uncle Pete. When their parents were alive they'd lived in a town house in the city with very modern decor. Uncle Pete never had a lick of decorating sense and truth be told, his house was never as clean as it was when Halle and Stella had lived there. He treated them like they were surrogates of Cinderella—dispersing chores and duties like they were payment for the privilege of living there and they'd better show their gratitude. Halle hadn't minded for the most part, since she was particular to living in a clean space. But Stella had despised Uncle Pete for the audacity.

"Mama and Daddy had good insurance policies," Stella said when they'd been sent to their rooms early one night. "So we shouldn't have to live in this dump with someone who doesn't even like us." Stella had been fed up and she'd sassed Uncle Pete. Halle had been punished as well, just in case she got any ideas to run her mouth like her sister.

"He could move us into a better house, back in the city. There was lots of money left over," Stella told her as they both lay across their twin beds on their stomachs. "I heard that lady, Ms. Joan, talking to the other lady, the one with the red hair that looks like Annie."

Halle grinned. "How is it you can remember all the movie characters' names, but can never remember a real live person's name? The other lady is Ms. Gwen. They both go to the church closer to town. At least, that's what she said when they came by with those cakes and cookies."

Stella flipped onto her back and rubbed a hand over her stomach. "That cake was so good. What did she say it was called again?"

"Kentucky butter cake," Halle told her. "And it was good. But I liked Mama's buttermilk pound cake better." Tears pooled in her eyes. "I'll never have that again."

Stella got off her bed then and came over to drop onto Halle's bed. She reached for her sister's hand and held it in her own. "You'll learn how to make Mama's pound cake. Uncle Pete has us in the kitchen cooking like we're sixteen-year-olds instead of ten-year-olds." She shook her head and the two ponytails she liked to style her hair in swooshed so that the loose hair slapped over her cheeks.

Halle preferred the neat look of two braids and so she did her hair that way. Uncle Pete didn't know how to do hair and probably wouldn't have done theirs if he could.

"It won't be like Mama's," Halle said, but she squeezed Stella's hand tightly. "Nothing's going to be the same again, is it, Stel?"

Stella shook her head. "Nope. It's not. But we'll make the best of it. We'll make it fun and then we'll leave and go have the best life ever!"

Adult Halle smiled at the memory. She could still hear Stella's voice—ten-year-old Stella and seventeen-year-old Stella. Whether she was talking or singing in that soulful alto timbre she had, there was nothing like her sister's voice. And never would be again. Halle was sure of that, just as she'd been certain that their lives wouldn't be the same once they moved to Blueridge. When Stella died, the thought that nothing in her world would be what it once was had almost broken her.

"How do I do this?" she spoke into the silence, her fingers clenched on the towel she'd picked up and wrapped around herself. "How do I do this again?"

It had taken what felt like all the strength she'd had to get over losing herself and being alone in a big city, but she'd done it. No, that was wrong. She hadn't done any of that on her own. In her weakest moments, which were many, the Lord had carried her. He'd been by her side, holding her up every day until she'd felt the strength slowly seeping back into her limbs, into her mind, into her heart. She'd prayed every day and trusted that He would bring her through, and He had.

"It's me again," she said in a low whisper. Then, right there in that bathroom, she bowed her head, closed her eyes and prayed.

Hours that felt like days later, she was awakened by the loud ringer on her phone. After the shower, and her talk with the Lord, Halle had lain across the queen-size bed in the center of the room for just a short nap. She and Tamera had taken Mr. James's advice and ate at the buffet once her bags arrived. So by the time she made it up to the room the shower had been the most pressing thing on her itinerary. The delicious food—pancakes, grits, home fries, cheesy scrambled eggs and the freshest fruit she'd seen on a buffet in a long time—coupled with that nice hot shower and the peace that can only come from giving all her burdens to the One who asked to carry them, had set the stage for the much-needed rest.

But Kyle's deep voice on the other end of the

phone snapped her awake as surely as if he'd dumped a bucket of cold water over her head.

"I'll be there in half an hour to pick you up," he said.

"Why? Where are we going?" she asked through a deep yawn.

"I told you we were going to Town Hall."

She nodded but stopped the second she realized he couldn't see her. "Yeah, you did. But that was this morning." Pulling the phone away from her ear, she spied the numbers on the screen. "It's almost four-thirty." Then her eyes widened. "What? It's almost four-thirty!"

She'd slept all afternoon.

"That means I'll be there at five. We'll go to Town Hall, take a look at what's in the time capsule, then decide how tonight's event will play out."

"Right," she said, now more focused. "Okay. That sounds like a good plan. I think."

"Stop thinking, Halle," he said. "Get dressed. I'll be there soon."

Then he disconnected the call and she frowned at the familiar way he continued to speak to her. As if all those years and all those unspoken words weren't still between them.

She pushed her arms into the jacket that matched the hunter green slacks she planned to wear to the banquet tonight. She had no idea

how long it would take to open the time capsule
and have the discussion Kyle wanted to have,
but the banquet was set to start at seven, so it
made sense to get dressed for it now. Once she
had the jacket on, she sat on the side of the bed
and reached for the platform-heeled black boo-
ties she'd packed. As she zipped each one, she
thought about Stella again. About what her sister
would say if she were here right now.

"That's not our class colors" would be Stella's
first complaint.

And she'd be right.

While Blueridge High School's colors were
navy blue and white, their graduating class had
taken a special vote to go with royal blue and
gold—or yellow as Kyle had argued the actual
color on their T-shirts was. Stella would've worn
those colors. A sassy little cocktail dress in royal
blue with shoes to match, a gold clutch, earrings
and chunky bracelet. Stella loved to dress up
and she adored jewelry. She loved vibrant colors and fun times.

Halle walked over to the dresser and stared at
herself in the mirror on top of it. She smoothed
down the lapels of the jacket, tilted her head at
the slight shimmer of the white blouse she wore
beneath it. Small gold hoops were at her ears and
she'd pulled out her flat iron to give her short

hair a little bump. She wore eyeliner, a little mas-
cara and buttercream gloss on her lips.

"No vibrancy, no fun," she said solemnly, then
shrugged. "You're not Stella. You never were."

That was something else she'd had to come
to terms with. Although that had started long
before Stella's or her parents' deaths. No, this
was an issue that had been with her since birth.
It had been decided for her that she'd be one of
two and she was basically okay with that, mostly
because nobody had warned her how much the
weight of expectancy would bear on her.

Stella was two minutes older and this year—
in June—she would've turned thirty-two with
Halle. Stella was the big sister. The fun sister. The vivacious sister. While Halle was the
younger sister. The serious sister. The boring
sister. Nobody ever said that; nobody that mattered, that is, but still, the words hung over Halle
like an unwanted halo. But not tonight.

With a shake of her head she declared, not
tonight.

While she'd come to this town to carry out one
of her sister's fondest wishes, she had no inten-
tion of going back to that place where she struggled to be good enough, even if only for herself.

So tonight she would go to that banquet wearing a color that didn't coordinate with this re-
uniting class, but she would do the thing they

all expected her to do. Then in the morning, she would pack her bags and go home. To the place where people knew only Halle and they expected her to be only who she'd always been.

The first thing Halle realized when Kyle picked her up dressed in his navy-blue uniform pants, matching shirt and the jacket she'd seen him in this morning, was that she was in big trouble. The kind of trouble that had nothing to do with the danger that might be lurking somewhere in this town. No, this was the kind of trouble a young girl's mother might've warned her about. The kind that didn't sneak around, but punched right in the gut and took her as a willing prisoner the second his deep brown eyes rested on her.

"Hey," he said as he stood inside the front entrance of the B&B. "You, uh… You look really good."

"Thanks," she replied. "You look…really professional. Is that what you're wearing to the banquet tonight?" That question came in a jumble of words that she hoped camouflaged how thankful she was that she hadn't just admitted he looked really good, too.

Although the words had been on the tip of her tongue. He looked, she allowed herself to admit for the second time in as many days, like a grown man. Not the teenager who'd shifted between being goofy and greedy, hogging all the snacks whenever they went to the movies and angry and sullen because nothing he did was ever good enough for his stern father.

Kyle looked down at himself, then lifted his head to stare at her once more. "I've been at the station interviewing witnesses all day," he said. "But I have my suit in the truck. Figured I'd change down at Town Hall when we're finished and then we could head over to the community center for the banquet."

"Oh." She nodded. "That makes sense. Guess I could've brought my clothes to change into as well."

"No," he replied. "I like what you're wearing."

And that shouldn't have made butterflies dance happily in her stomach. It shouldn't have lifted the corners of her mouth into a smile.

"So, we should go," she said abruptly. Then she set her purse next to a potted plant on one of three matching tables in the foyer. She had draped her black wool coat over an arm as she walked down the stairs, and now she lifted it to put it on.

Before she could, Kyle was behind her. He took the coat, held it so she could ease one arm in and then the other.

"Thanks," she said and pulled the coat around herself to button it.

"You're welcome," he replied.

They didn't speak again until she was seat-belted into the passenger seat of his truck. This one wasn't the town-issued sheriff's vehicle. Even though he was still wearing his uniform—complete with the shiny badge and duty belt—Kyle had obviously switched to his personal vehicle—a matte gray Dodge Ram. It smelled like him in here, like the heavy sandalwood notes of whatever cologne he wore.

"Cool Water," she said and chuckled. Then, because she hadn't realized she'd said it out loud, she gasped and clapped her lips shut.

"What did you just say?"

Of course, he'd heard her. If there was a way she could embarrass herself, Halle always found it.

She sighed and shook her head. "I was just recalling you used to love Cool Water cologne. You would put on so much I could smell you before you even stepped onto our front porch."

He laughed. A deep, hearty laugh that had his mouth opening wide, his eyes crinkling with humor. She'd missed that sound.

"Wow, you remember that?" he asked as his hands gripped the steering wheel and he made a left turn.

She nodded. "I do," she said. "You smell different now." Bolder, she thought. More confident.

"I make more money now. I can afford better cologne," he replied.

"Right." She looked out the window at the storefronts, some old and some new, and hoped to discover something more interesting than this conversation and the man who sat across from her.

"Well, do you like this cologne?" he asked. "I remember you always wanted to wear my hoodies and jackets because you said they smelled good like me."

Her cheeks warmed and she clasped her fingers together on her lap. Of course, he would remember that part. "Uh, it's okay." Why she couldn't just admit to him that she liked this new scent, a lot, she had no clue.

"Is the rest of your team going to meet us at Town Hall?" she asked because she desperately needed to stop this little trip down memory lane. "Tamera could've just gotten a ride with us."

"No," he said. If he thought the shift in topic was odd, he didn't mention it. Maybe he didn't want to remember their past, either. It hadn't always been pleasant for him. "They're gathering some facts back at the station."

"Oh," she said quietly. "Why did you call them here? I mean, you don't even know what's going on, and wouldn't this have to be some type of federal case to bring them in?"

"Local authorities can invite the FBI to assist in cold cases," he said. "In this particular instance, it's more like they're honoring a favor from the past."

He made another turn and before she could ask her next question, he added, "I never stopped looking for Stella's killer."

Halle continued to stare out the window.

"Once I landed at the FBI, I knew I wanted to take a look at the case from a different angle. From the lens of an adult, a trained investigator and profiler," he said.

"But you had other cases," she said. "You were supposed to do your job."

"My job was to put violent criminals behind bars," he said. "Whoever killed Stella was... *is*...a violent criminal."

Her head jerked in his direction. "You think whoever killed Stella is still alive? That he's still in Blueridge?"

He stopped at a traffic light and looked over to her. "I think there's a connection. Between you, the time capsule and what happened to Stella."

EIGHT

Kyle didn't visit Town Hall as frequently as some of the council members would have preferred. In fact, he didn't do a lot of the things Heath had done that the council members had expected him to do as well. But when Kyle decided to run in the special election to fill the position long held by his father, he'd done so knowing he'd make some changes. Not necessarily in how the sheriff's department kept the citizens of Blueridge safe, but more in dismantling antiquated procedures that were no longer efficient.

The monthly meeting where the seven-member council expected him to run down every person he'd arrested, written a citation for, or even given a warning for jaywalking, wasn't efficient. A written report emailed to each council member made more sense than the two-hour session filled with coffee, donuts and enough town gossip to make it as annoying as it was a time-suck.

"Hey there, Kyle." Emma, the first-floor receptionist, spoke as he entered the building right behind Halle.

"Hi, Emma," he said and returned the warm smile Emma always offered when he was here. Emma had graduated with Brian, so she was in her late twenties. She'd married right out of high school but had divorced two years later and now she lived over on Millers Way, with her grandmother and her eight-year-old son, Malcolm.

"Emma, this is Halle Jefferson. Not sure if you remember her, since you were a few years behind us in school," he said when they stepped up to the glossed front desk.

Emma's smile remained intact as she shifted her gaze to Halle.

"I sure do remember her," Emma said. "Your sister, Stella, braided my hair for my eighth-grade graduation."

Halle smiled easily. If the mention of Stella—so soon after he'd told her he thought there was a connection to Stella's death and what was going on now—was bothering her, he couldn't tell.

"Yes," Halle said. "I remember you, too. You looked so pretty that day and you loved your hair."

"I did," Emma said and lifted her fingers to the bone-straight shoulder-length brown strands she now wore. "I loved how neat and pretty they looked. Everybody in town wanted Stella to braid their hair after that."

"I know," Halle replied. "She made a good amount of money doing hair that summer."

"I called Spence earlier and told him we were coming down. He said he'd leave everything we needed in one of the conference rooms." The sooner they got this over with, the better. Halle seemed to be handling things well, but he knew that would only last for so long.

"Oh, okay. Well, you know his office is on the second floor. So, he's probably talking about one of the rooms up there. Just go on up and I'll tell Lynn you're on your way." Emma picked up her phone and put it to her ear. Then she looked at Halle. "It's so nice seeing you back in town, Halle."

"Thanks," Halle said. "It's nice seeing you again, too."

He noted she didn't say it was nice being back in town, but after all she'd been through, he couldn't blame her.

They were quiet on the elevator and as they walked down the hallway toward the office of Spencer Roman, the youngest member on the council.

"Halle Jefferson!" Spence's administrative assistant squealed as she popped up from her desk, which was positioned directly in front of Spence's office door. "Girl, come here and give me a hug. It's so good to see you!"

Before Halle could decide whether she wanted a hug or not, Lynn had skirted around the desk and wrapped her arms around her. For an instant Halle didn't respond, then she pressed her hands tentatively to Lynn's back and said, "Hi, Lynn. It's good to see you."

Lynn held the embrace, gave Halle a little side-to-side shake before finally letting her go. "You look so good," Lynn said and took a step back to look Halle up and down. "That's a sharp coat and those boots. Plus, you always were pretty. Like that real quiet kind of elegant pretty. Whereas Stella just grabbed you in the throat with her beauty."

"They were identical twins, Lynn," he said because he noticed Halle's slight flinch at the woman's words.

Lynn waved a hand at him. "I know. I know," she said. "But you know what I mean. Stella had all the flash and Halle here, she had the quiet allure."

"Thanks, Lynn," Halle said. "Can you direct us to the conference room? We're on a tight schedule."

"Oh. Okay." Lynn frowned, undoubtedly ruffled by Halle's cool request.

Kyle was proud as he looped his thumbs in his front pockets and waited.

"Let me just look on the schedule here," Lynn said as she went back around her desk and stared into a date book. "Spence had to get over to the community center—they needed a few more hands to set up the lighting for tonight's event. You know since everything had to be moved from the resort. I'm surprised they didn't call you, Kyle. Most of the other classmates, the ones from the basketball and football teams, have been drafted to help with all sorts of stuff this week."

"I know," he replied. "I've received a few emails from the alumni committee. Already have my assignments."

"Oh, all right. 'Cause you know everybody should have to pull their weight, even if you're wearing that big sparkly badge." Lynn looked up at them with a sweet smile. "You're in conference room B. Straight down that way, at the end of the hall."

"Thanks," he told her and reached for Halle's hand.

She took it and they walked down the hall, neither of them turning back, even though they knew Lynn was staring at them. Waiting for the moment they disappeared into the conference room so she could hop on her phone and call anyone in town who would listen to the gossip that Kyle and Halle were holding hands and probably together again.

That thought didn't annoy him as much as it should have.

He watched Halle remove her coat, fold it once and lay it almost gingerly over the back of a chair. At the farthest end of the long mahogany table, close to the back wall of the conference room, sat the clear case that was at the resort last night. She rubbed her palms up and down her legs as she stood at the other end of the table, staring down at it.

"I still have the key," he said. "I told Spence we needed to see what was inside. Try to figure out what this guy who texted you wanted."

She nodded slowly. "I know everything she put in there," she said. "I wasn't on their committee, didn't want to be because—"

"Because you wanted some separation." He finished for her. "After seventeen years of being her twin, you wanted some separation. Even if it was just this one thing."

She turned to look up at him. "You remember?"

He nodded. "I do."

It had taken a lot for her to tell Stella she didn't want to be on the senior class committee. Was she a part of the graduating class? Sure, just like the other one hundred and five students. But that hadn't meant she needed to sit beside her sister, who'd been unanimously voted president, and make plans for their last year at Blueridge High. So she hadn't. And Kyle had never been prouder of her than in that moment, because he knew how much taking that small bit of independence meant to her.

"I haven't thought about this thing in years," she said as she started walking toward the other end of the table. "When we locked it away, I didn't plan to think about it again until… I guess now."

"To tell the truth, I hadn't thought about it, either," he said. "Until I started receiving those emails about the reunion."

He closed the door and pushed the lock into place. He didn't want them to be disturbed, nor did he want anyone to overhear what they were talking about. As an added precaution, he crossed the room to close the blinds at the window behind the table.

"That one with the newspaper article and the picture of Stella and the entire committee standing beside the capsule," he continued as he removed his jacket and draped it on a chair. "It brought back a lot of memories."

"For me, too," Halle said. She finally stopped

walking and gripped the back of a chair, keeping space between herself and the time capsule.

It was odd-looking in that it wasn't exactly shaped like a capsule. Instead, it looked like one of those old miniature tabletop clocks, but with a deep base, covered in blue felt, where all the items were housed. Their graduating year was embroidered along the front of the base, in a yellow block font.

"Everybody looked so happy in that picture," she said. "Stella was ecstatic. She loved the idea of the time capsule. Loved that it would be her last project before we'd be getting on a bus and leaving this town. It was closer to drive over to Morgantown and fly into Dulles or get a direct flight to New York, but we wanted to spend a day in Baltimore, visit our parents' graves first." She paused and shook her head slowly, like the memory might've been getting too hard.

"Then catching a flight from BWI to Laguardia and from there the two of you would head to the apartment your scholarship would partially pay for, and I would find a hotel until I could get a job and a permanent place to stay." He sighed with the thought. "I saved most of my paychecks and all of my tips from working at the crab house so that I'd have enough to stay afloat until I found a job." And he'd planned to live off peanut butter and jelly sandwiches and water bottles he'd buy in bulk until then.

It shocked him to realize that she'd looked away from the time capsule to stare at him. "It sounded like such a good plan back then."

There were questions in her eyes and something that felt like regret. He didn't want to address either. Didn't want to have this conversation that was a long time coming.

He reached into his pocket and pulled out the key he'd taken from the hall last night.

"Let's see what we've got," he said and moved closer.

Halle remained still.

He inserted the key into the lock at the back of the base and turned until there was a click and the lock popped open.

Then he glanced up at Halle. "Ready?"

She inhaled deeply, her fingers clenching the back of the chair. When she released the breath, she nodded and said, "Ready."

The capsule opened from the back, so he tilted it, laying it down on the blue base, then pulled each side apart. The fifteen-year-old contents remained folded and tucked into one side. He began to pull them out.

"The newspaper clipping," he said. "From when that reporter came out to the first rehearsal for the graduation ceremony."

"Troy Hamilton was the photographer for the school paper and his father, Jet, worked at the *Blue Times* as an editor," Halle said.

"Yup. Troy owns a photography studio a few blocks from here. He does a lot of wedding photography over at the resort and some stock stuff that he says makes most of his money throughout the year." He unfolded the article and set it to the side.

There was another folded piece of paper on top of the article.

"It's Stella's speech," she said when he unfolded it. "The one she gave when she'd taken office as class president."

He read a couple of lines and grinned. "Stella was a funny girl."

"Yeah," Halle replied. "She was. Those jokes just came naturally and they weren't corny at all. You know I would've told her if they were."

He gave a wry chuckle. "I know you would have."

"Well, I wasn't going to let my sister embarrass herself," she added and then sighed. "Aww, it's Grizzie."

Kyle frowned as he held the brown stuffed animal in his hand. "You named the school mascot Grizzie?"

She shrugged. "He's a grizzly bear, what else would we name him?"

"So glad you never told me that," he said and grinned. "Debate club wins first place in the regional championship." He held up the white-and-gold ribbon, set it down then picked up the keychain. "Senior prom favor. And a bunch of pictures."

"Fifteen pictures," she said. "One for each year the capsule would be locked away. Stella thought that was a cute idea."

He shrugged. "She would think that."

Because he wasn't certain Halle was going to move from that spot, Kyle laid each picture on the table in three rows of five.

"Random pictures from events we did throughout senior year," she said. "None of this looks like something someone would kill for. Unless they just wanted to kill me like they did Stella." She yanked her hands away from the chair. "That's what you're thinking, isn't it? That I'm a target now. I came all the way back to this stupid, cold town where I never wanted to be. I lose my sister here and yet I still make the decision to put my career on hold and come back here and for what? To fulfill my sister's wishes or to die so I can be buried in a grave beside her?"

"Stop it," Kyle said and clapped his hands on her shoulders. He turned her to face him. "Just stop it!" He'd been waiting for this moment, had known it was bound to come and was glad it had come at a time when they were alone.

No way did he want anyone else seeing her fall apart. Especially not when he was almost positive that the shooter was someone who lived in Blueridge.

"They weren't shooting at you last night," he said when she had stopped talking but was shaking her head, her entire body trembling. "They were shooting at me!"

"Wha...what?" She looked up at him, eyes blinking furiously as they always did when she was upset. "What did you just say?"

"It was me he was aiming at, not you," he said evenly. "He needed you to open the time capsule. Even if you didn't do it last night, the plan was always for you to open it. That's what the alumni committee wanted and even if he'd been successful in getting me out of the way, the ceremony would've eventually been rescheduled and they would call on you again to open it."

"I don't understand," she said on a gasp. "None of this makes sense, Kyle. There's nothing in there that would make somebody want to kill for it. Nothing!"

He couldn't help but glance back at the table. "You're right. I don't see anything that would be worth it, but that's probably because we don't know who he is. That's what my team's working on now. Trying to come up with enough clues to get a preliminary profile. Once we know who he is we can figure out what he wants."

"What he wants is what we just did," she said and backed out of his grasp. "He wanted me to get this key and open the capsule before tonight's event, I'm guessing. Maybe he wanted to see what was in it without anyone else being around. So, he would've asked me to bring it to him."

She walked over to the window, her back to him as she talked. Then turned to face him again and folded her arms over her chest.

"Probably," he said.

"And I would've gone because I was afraid and confused and I just wanted all of this to be over." She tilted her head back then and closed her eyes. "I thought it was over fifteen years ago."

"So did I," he replied and resisted the urge to go to her, to take her in his arms once more. To comfort her and promise her…whatever…to do whatever he could to make her feel whole and safe again.

For endless moments they stood there staring at each other until she finally asked, "What do we do now?"

Now, this was something he could handle. It was something he could actually do instead of standing there feeling utterly helpless. He still cared about her, deeply. If he was in the mood to be really honest and pull back all the layers of anger, regret and disappointment he'd wrapped himself in all these years, he would admit that he was still in love with her. But the reality was Halle wasn't back in Blueridge to stay. She was leaving, tomorrow, she'd said. And in this moment, he wasn't any more prepared to give her the love and the life she deserved than he had been fifteen years ago.

"We continue investigating," he said. "We go to that banquet tonight and act like nothing is wrong. I'll get Brian and the rest of my team down here and you'll open that time capsule, just like planned."

"And that'll do what? Entice him to come for me again?" she asked. "You think he's gonna text me tonight the way he did last night?"

Kyle rubbed a finger over his chin. "I'm actually surprised he hasn't done that already. You didn't do what he told you to last night. He was angry—that's why he shot through that window and at my truck this morning."

"Great, so we've made him mad. How is that helpful?"

"If he's angry, he'll be off his game. He'll make a mistake." Looking back at the items from the time capsule, Kyle wondered if he hadn't already made one. "When he does, we'll be there to catch him."

"I don't know why this is happening," she said, her voice hitching.

"It's nothing you did and nothing Stella did. He is the only one responsible for what's happening, Halle. You have to believe that," Kyle told her, his tone unwavering.

She let her hands fall to her sides and she walked back to the table. "I know it's nothing I've done," she said. "I don't know who this is or what his gripe is with me or was with Stella, but if this is the only way he thinks he can settle it, then, I guess we'll just have to stop him."

When his lips spread into a grin, he wondered if it was appropriate for this moment and these circumstances. But then Halle looked up and gave him a small smile in return. "So, you're up, Mr. Sheriff. Tell me how you plan to catch this guy."

Kyle was just about to reply when thumping sounded at the door.

"Kyle Briscoe, you open up this door right now!" a woman yelled from outside the room. "I know you're in there with little miss Halle Jefferson."

At those last snidely spoken words, Kyle knew exactly who was on the other side of the door.

And from the quick roll of Halle's eyes, she knew, too.

"I'll put the stuff back inside," she told him and started refolding the speech and the newspaper clipping.

"Just a second," Kyle yelled, knowing that would only infuriate their surprise guest even more.

"Don't you *just a second* me! My tax dollars pay your salary and I'll have you booted out of that office so fast your daddy's head will turn in his grave."

Kyle frowned at that last remark and reminded himself he'd been taught not to put his hands on girls. Or women with vicious mouths and cotton for brains. When he'd helped Halle get the last of the items back into the capsule, he handed her the lock and slipped the key into his pocket. Then he walked casually to the door.

After unlocking it, he pulled the door open slowly. "What can I do for you, Marcia?"

Marcia Delaney-Hightower stormed into the conference room, a scowl on what he considered a marginally pretty face—if she wasn't always saying or doing something mean and unnecessary. The way a person's personality could make them unattractive was still astounding to him.

"I can't believe the two of you have found the time to meet up and start trading secrets with all that's just happened." Hands on both her hips now, Marcia's black handbag swung at her wrist.

She was about five foot two or three, shorter than Halle's five foot seven, but that didn't prevent her from marching right over to where Halle stood and stopping just barely a foot away. "And you haven't been back in town for a hot second and you're already starting up gossip."

"Considering I've only spoken to the sheriff and Mr. James in the two days I've been here, I'm not sure how much gossip I could be starting," Halle replied.

She'd locked the time capsule again and placed the clear covering over it.

"Smart-mouthed, just like always," Marcia continued. "And I heard about what happened last night. One minute you were there at the mixer and the next you weren't."

"Oh, I thought you were speaking about the fact that someone shot into the ballroom," Halle said. "That seems like the bigger news to me."

Marcia huffed and was about to say something else, when Kyle thought it was time to end this encounter.

"Marcia, you're interrupting official business. Now, unless you have something important you need to say here…" He let his voice trail off. Then he snapped his fingers. "Oh, I know why you're in such a hurry to talk to me. You forgot to come down to the station like I instructed you to do last night. You want to give me your statement now."

She lifted a hand, and the huge pear-shaped diamond that Robert Hightower, owner of Blueridge's only auto body shop, had put on her finger glistened beneath the fluorescent lights. How many years had Rob had a crush on Marcia and how many years had Marcia treated him like a wad of gum on the bottom of her shoe? Kyle was shocked and concerned when he'd learned they'd been married for the past eight years and had two daughters.

Marcia tucked a neat curl behind her ear and turned her root beer-brown gaze toward him. "Like I told your little deputy last night, I didn't see anything. I was in the ladies' room, came out to a lot of screaming and running, so I did the same. And since you thought I was going to stand outside and freeze to death last night, I needed a trip back to the resort for some time in the sauna this morning."

"I need your official statement in writing and signed, Marcia. Get yourself into the station to make that happen in the next twenty-four hours, or I'll have to send a deputy to your house to pick you up," he said, then reached for his coat.

"You wouldn't dare!" She narrowed her eyes.

"Try me," he replied. "Now, if you'll excuse

us, Halle and I need to get ready for the banquet. You are coming tonight, aren't you? I know it was a hassle moving it from the resort down to the community center, but considering all that's going on, I'm sure you agreed with the rest of the committee that was for the best."

"You mean since you declared the ballroom a crime scene and won't allow us to have the banquet at the resort tonight," she said with another huff. "Yes, I'll be there. And she should be there on time. The sooner we get this over with, the sooner we can get on with the rest of the week's festivities."

"I agree," Halle said. "I'd like to get this over with as well."

With pursed lips, Marcia tossed Halle an annoyed look over her shoulder. "I'm sure you would, so you can get back to your high and mighty lifestyle in New York."

"You're absolutely right," was Halle's quick retort before she grabbed her coat and put it on.

Kyle hadn't needed the reminder that Marcia and Halle weren't long-lost friends. Even though Marcia's true gripe had always been with Stella, since she was jealous of any and everything Stella ever had. But by default, he supposed, Marcia didn't like Halle, either. And Halle had never seemed to care. Still, he could've done without Marcia's reminding him that Halle was leaving soon.

While his mind might have a grip on what this reunion really meant, his heart was having a hard time accepting that there would be no second chance with him and the only woman he'd ever loved.

NINE

The Geraldine Wright Community Center was lit up with what seemed like every twinkle light in town. They were hanging from the ceiling, wrapped around columns, and filling the crystal vases set in the center of each table. Every chair was covered in the same blue satin that draped each round table. Gold chargers with white plates and a perfectly folded blue napkin marked each guest's spot, along with a larger than necessary name card.

"Oh joy, I'm at the head table," Halle said dryly after she walked the entire room in search of her name. "Along with what looks like everyone who was on the senior class committee." They were early, so besides the catering staff who were in and out of the main room and the kitchen in the back, they were the only ones here.

"Marcia's sitting right next to the mayor, of course," Brian said. He and Kyle had changed out of their uniforms and now wore very dapper-looking black suits.

"She was the class secretary, right?" Tamera said. She also wore a pantsuit, like Halle, but in a formal black that Halle figured was part of her official uniform.

"Begrudgingly so," Halle replied. "Stella won the president spot and Marcia had one of her signature—yet still embarrassing—tantrums. So, our class adviser, Ms. Pennyworth, put her in the secretary position since nobody volunteered for that job."

Tamera nodded and continued to walk the length of the rectangular head table. "Yeah, we have her on the list of Stella's enemies."

Kyle mentioned that his team was working on figuring out what the shooter really wanted, but he didn't say that would include making lists about Stella. Or was that more of the victimology he'd mentioned? If they were thinking that last night's events were connected to what happened fifteen years ago, then it stood to reason that Stella was being considered a victim as well.

"Emily Cason, treasurer, and Aaron Barkley, vice president," Tamera said as she passed each seat. She didn't pull out a small notepad to write down every clue she found or fact she wanted to remember. That must be something they only did on those television procedural shows.

There was another rectangular table and a podium in the center, between the two. Tamera
and Najee continued walking and checking place
cards.

"We've got Principal Gibson, Rosalee Hodges—
same last name as the mayor. His wife?" Najee
asked.

"Yeah," Kyle replied. He stayed on the other
side of the head tables, surveying the rest of the
room while they were focused here.

Glancing up at him now, Halle wondered what
he was thinking. She'd thought he looked nice,
mature and very handsome in his sheriff's uniform, but dressed in this suit with that crisp
white shirt and royal blue tie, he looked like
he'd just stepped off the cover of *GQ* magazine.

"Nathaniel Hodges was on the town council
when we were in high school. Married Rosalee,
whose father owns the diner over on Banner
Road, and moved up the ranks until he won the
mayoral election three years ago," Kyle said and
turned to face them.

Halle immediately looked down at the table
again. She wasn't here to gawk at her ex. Tonight was about fulfilling her sister's wish and
hopefully finding something that would lead
Kyle and his team to that shooter. She planned
to focus her mind on the former for the time
being.

When her phone rang loudly, she hurriedly unsnapped her purse and dug it out. Everyone in the room seemed to stop still while she stared down at the screen. "It's my manager," she said and moved away from the table.

"Hi, Stefan," she answered when she was a few tables away from the others.

"Hello to you, darlin'. How's it going down there in winterland?" Stefan had a cheerful Southern drawl that always struck her as out of place in New York. He was her height with a good-looking round face and a love of shoes that almost rivaled hers.

"Oh, it's going," was her drab response.

"That bad, huh?"

He had absolutely no idea and she wasn't about to tell him. "It's what it was fifteen years ago." That wasn't a lie.

"Well, I've got the schedule finalized. Press releases and announcements are being crafted as I speak. We'll be ready to publicly announce the tour on Monday." She could hear him clapping his hands. "Kaitlyn's talking to the people at the *Today* show, trying to nail down a date in the next couple of weeks so we can get you in before you leave for the first show in Boston."

"Right," she said. The tour had been the last thing on her mind today. "That…uh, it sounds good."

"Hey. You okay? Your old classmates workin' your nerves already?" he asked.

Again, if he only knew.

"It's just a lot," she admitted. "I figured it would be and now that I'm here, it's a reality."

"But it's almost over," he said. "You'll be out of there first thing tomorrow morning, right? What time's your flight again?"

She was flying out of Morgantown this time, going directly to Dulles to catch her connecting flight back to New York. "It's at noon. My taxi is scheduled to pick me up at seven in the morning so I'll make it to the airport in time."

"Fantastic! You'll be home by dinnertime. I'll make us a late reservation at Maggie's. You love their lasagna. I hate that meat sauce with a passion, but the shrimp scampi is divine. We'll have champagne and—"

"Hey," Kyle whispered as he tapped her on the shoulder. "We're going to sit right over here. Join us when you're done."

She looked up to see him standing beside her. Stefan yelled her name through the phone and Kyle raised a brow.

"Sure," she said hurriedly. "I'll be right there."

And before she could wait for another reaction from Kyle, she returned her attention to Stefan. "I'm here. I'm here," she said. "Yes, dinner sounds fine."

"Oh, chile, I thought you'd lost your signal in those mountains," Stefan continued. "So, I'll send a car to pick you up at the airport. You know I hate driving in the city."

"You never leave the city," she said glibly.

"Because I love it here," was his comeback, in a tone that said she should've known that would be the reply.

With a half smile, she said, "I'll see you to-morrow night, Stefan."

"Yes, right. Take care of yourself and hurry home, darlin'."

Halle ended the call and dropped the phone back into her purse. As she started walking toward the table where Kyle and the rest of his team were sitting, she heard loud voices and footsteps. Marcia and a couple other women had arrived.

"I don't know how I'm going to survive the night sitting up there with her," Halle said when she made it to the table.

"You won't have to," Kyle replied and pointed to the name card to the right of where he sat.

She grinned. "Oooohhhh, you're gonna get it. You can't just move name cards." She sat down anyway, like she believed for one minute they'd be caught and really get into some type of trouble.

"Nobody's gonna notice," Brian said.

Halle shook her head. "Marcia will notice. She

hates me, so she'll take every opportunity to put me in what she thinks is my place."

"The list of enemies for you and your sister isn't actually that long," Najee said from across the table. He wore a black suit, too, but he completed his secret-agent look with a black shirt and no tie. He was sort of giving her mafia vibes with the medium-size diamond stud in his left ear. Either that or retired NBA player. He continued, "Considering the two of you were extremely popular and pretty. That's usually the perfect recipe for a gang of haters."

Halle removed her coat and hung it over the back of her chair. "Oh, gracious, I sure hope we weren't walking around with a gang of haters," she replied with a chuckle.

"We're looking for a classmate," Tamera added solemnly. She stared at the doorway now, watching as a few more people came in. "Someone who knew you and Stella and knew about the time capsule."

Kyle sat back in his chair. On the surface he looked casual enough but tension was rolling off him in waves, reaching out to engulf her as she sat beside him. "That would be the entire class. And there was nothing in that capsule worth killing for."

"I agree," she said. "All I felt from those items was heavy nostalgia."

"There's something in that nostalgia," Tamera continued. "Something he wants. Maybe needs."

"Then why wouldn't he have just walked into the ballroom and snatched it last night?" Brian asked.

"Too many people watching," Najee replied. "Where was the capsule kept all this time?"

"In the basement of Town Hall," Kyle said. "Spence told me it was locked in a vault down there with some historical artifacts."

Tamera frowned. "That's pretty intense for a time capsule that's full of nostalgia for a bunch of high school kids."

"We're a small town," Kyle replied with a shrug. "That time capsule and all the attention Stella and the committee drummed up for it was the biggest thing happening in town that year."

"Well, that and the debate team bringing home the first-place trophy. Our sports teams might not have been top-tier, but the debate team and the band got us a lot of recognition back then," Brian said. "And my aunt Josephine said that kind of stuff brought in money."

"Aaron Barkley." She blinked as if when she opened her eyes again he wouldn't be there. But he was. Dressed in a smoky gray suit and shirt and a navy-blue tie, he walked up to the head table and took his seat. Marcia had been across the room talking to someone but now she was heading back to the head table as well.

"Together again," Kyle said blandly.

"Again? A couple?" Najee looked up, interested.

"Marcia had the biggest crush on Aaron and she made no secret about it," Brian said. "But Stella got him first."

"Marcia's at the top of that list for enemies so far," Tamera said.

Kyle shook his head. "They both had alibis for the night of the murder," he said. "Though Marcia gave a flimsy statement about last night when we saw her at Town Hall a little while ago."

"Aaron just came into town this morning," a guy who was built like a linebacker said as he stepped up to the table. "I heard Marcia drove up to Morgantown to pick him up first thing this morning. Took Rob's truck to do it, too."

Brian shook his head. "How do you take your husband's truck to pick up your ex-boyfriend?"

"That's what I said," replied the big guy, who was starting to look even more familiar. "But you know, Rob's had hearts in his eyes for Marcia since we were all running around the playground in elementary school." His gaze landed on Halle and he smiled. "Pardon my manners," he said. "Welcome home, Twin."

She tilted her head, recognized the dimple in

his left cheek and smiled back. "Spencer Roman. You're still the only one I'll allow to call me that." He had changed a lot since their high school years. Not only the fifty or so pounds he looked to have gained, but also the beard and receding hairline. She remembered when they were young, he'd worn his hair faded on the sides and three to four inches long on top.

"Of course I'm the only one—I was your first friend here in Blueridge. Took you and Twin around to meet everybody who was anybody. I earned that right," Spence said.

She chuckled. He called both her and Stella Twin like he couldn't come up with anything more original. And while the name had stuck with him, Spence had never allowed anyone else to get away with calling them that. He'd lived across the street from Uncle Pete's house and had been like the big brother that she and Stella never had.

"So, wait? Marcia and Aaron did end up becoming a couple? Somewhere in the file it mentioned Aaron as Stella's boyfriend," Najee continued, totally ignoring the mini-reunion that just took place.

"He was," Halle said. "For about a year and a half. All of junior year and the beginning of senior year. Stella broke it off with him right before Valentine's Day."

Spence nodded. "And Marcia swooped right in to claim him."

"But I didn't think they'd gotten together," Halle said. "Because Aaron never stopped calling or coming over to our house to see Stella. Even the night of graduation he'd wanted to talk to her again and she'd agreed. But she was never getting back with him, especially since we were heading to New York."

"Interesting," Tamera said and arched a brow.

Kyle shook his head. "Aaron and Marcia were together at the time of the murder. My dad talked to both of them. He said Aaron was a little embarrassed to admit Marcia had snuck him into the Delaneys' house late that night after the party."

"Yeah, but Marcia had been ecstatic to claim him," Brian added. "They were a hot item for a few months after that."

Before anyone could speak again, Marcia stood at the podium and tapped on the microphone. "Good evening, fellow grizzlies!" She didn't need that microphone at all, as loud as her natural voice was. But she continued, leading the crowd into the pep rally chant as her way of beginning the program.

"Stella loved planning things." Halle smiled as she stood behind the podium and spoke.

She'd always had a beautiful smile. Truth be told, there was never anything about her Kyle hadn't found wonderfully alluring. She enjoyed reading as much as she loved music, and a few summer nights when his friends were out sneaking beers or getting into some other type of trouble, he recalled lying on a blanket in the grass listening while she used her flashlight to read from some book. He wondered if she knew those were the nights she saved him.

"For our twelfth birthday she planned a movie marathon, but we had to dress up like dancers because the theme was 'dance the night away' and all the movies we watched featured dancers or some connection to dance." Halle paused, lifted a finger to place just beneath her nose as she closed her eyes briefly and tried not to cry.

Kyle inhaled deeply, attempting to keep his own feelings in check. There'd been so many emotions sifting through him since he'd learned she was coming back to town—elation, nervousness, sadness, optimism. They all swirled in a funnel when he saw her last night. And now, with all that was going on, it was a struggle to hold his expectations in line.

"It might sound silly to all of you," she continued, "now that we're grown. But to me that will always be the best birthday ever." She stood a little straighter now, her shoulders squared. "My sister is gone but this part of her legacy will live on. She loved the idea of this project, of preserving our past and, at measured intervals, introducing it to our present. All in an effort to leave a mark on our future." Another steadying breath and a small smile. "It is in that spirit that I have the honor of opening the time capsule we sealed fifteen years ago and adding a few new items."

There was applause from the crowd and Marcia hurriedly stood, offering a blue velour bag to Halle. The smile that was pasted on Marcia's face was as phony as a three-dollar bill. Mayor Hodges stood as well, his smile more genuine.

"The alumni committee curated these items to be put into the capsule," Marcia said. "We're certain our beloved class president would've agreed with the selections."

"She's something else, isn't she?" Tamera asked, leaning over from where she sat to Kyle's left.

"And this is the mature version of her," he said, not wanting to recall all the gossip and drama Marcia used to keep going around town.

"This," Marcia said, holding up an 8x10 picture that anyone who wasn't sitting at the head table couldn't see, "is the next graduating class of Blueridge High School. The future of Blueridge as Principal Gibson used to tell us."

There was more laughter from the crowd.

Even Principal Gibson with his full gray beard and afro chuckled.

Marcia handed the picture to Halle and Halle placed it on top of the other items that were already in the time capsule. They'd agreed that she wouldn't take out the individual items tonight. Going on their profile that the unsub was a classmate, there was a good chance he would be here. He would want to keep a close eye on what was going on, closer than his hideaway in the trees last night. That was why Kyle wanted Brian and the rest of the team here. If anything went down, he wanted to be prepared.

"And this beauty right here," Marcia said, holding up the next item, "is the invitation I personally designed for this week's reunion festivities." She flipped the navy blue 5x7 invite over. "As you all may know it has our schedule for this week printed on the back. That'll be so much fun to look back on in another fifteen years."

This time, a low rumble of boos came from the far left corner of the room and Marcia scowled.

Mayor Hodges cleared his throat and leaned a little closer to the mic. At this point, Halle appeared trapped between the two who both wanted to be heard. She took the invitation from Marcia and set it on top of the time capsule.

"On behalf of the town council and myself, Nathaniel Randall Hodges, the third, mayor of

the great town of Blueridge, we present this citation in honor of a bright light that was taken
away from us far too soon. From this day forward, today will officially be known as Stella
Ann Jefferson day."

Applause was loud throughout the room. Two
people he recognized as former teachers stood
up and others began to pop up, too, until just
about everyone was standing. At their table,
Tamera stood, Kyle followed and then Najee
and Brian. Each of them continued to peruse
the room, looking for who hadn't stood, was
Kyle's guess.

Would the unsub remain seated? Would his
anger over last night's failed attempt to get to the
capsule be eating him up? Or was he watching,
calmly, waiting for his next opening to…what?
What was his endgame?

"Nobody looks out of place," Najee said.

"Because they all belong here," Kyle replied.
"They all grew up here. That's going to make
singling him out a little harder." He hated to
admit that, but it was a fact.

"Until he messes up," Tamera said, just as
Mayor Hodges began to speak again.

Kyle was about to take his seat when someone
tapped him on his shoulder. "Hey, Sheriff." It
was Eddie Bateman, one of the security guards
from Town Hall. "We've got a problem."

TEN

Marcia grabbed Halle's arm just as she was about to step away from the head table.

"You always thought you were better than us," she said when Halle turned back to look at her.

Halle yanked her arm from Marcia's grasp. "It never took much effort to be better than someone as petty and unhappy as you, Marcia. But I prayed for you every Sunday regardless."

Her makeup was flawless, her hair in perfect barrel curls that fell softly around a face that would be very pretty if she wasn't in such a surly mood all the time. That was what Ms. Joan, who was also one of the senior ushers at church, used to say. No matter what was going on, what she had or didn't have, Marcia never seemed to be content. It was unfortunate for Stella and Halle that the majority of the time Marcia blamed them for that.

"Save your prayers," Marcia snapped. "I don't need them. And we don't need you here. Kyle doesn't need you. He's been doing good since he came back. Getting over his daddy's death and taking his rightful place as sheriff. Then you blow into town and the next thing you know people are shooting and there's screaming and running. Poor Noel couldn't even make it here tonight and he was supposed to do some of those magic tricks he used to do in school."

It took everything in Halle not to comment on Noel's horrendous magic skills, or to admit that this wasn't exactly where she wanted to be right now, either. "Calm down, Marcia. You don't have to get yourself all worked up. I'm leaving—"

Halle never finished the sentence because she and Marcia were joined by another classmate.

"Halle," he said and reached for her hand. "It's so wonderful to see you again. I've missed seeing you here in town."

His hand was clammy against hers and he gripped it tight. "Freddie," she said and told herself it would be rude to yank her hand from his, the way she'd yanked her arm from Marcia just moments ago.

But seriously, what was up with this random touching and people being in her space without permission? If she wasn't already feeling overwhelmed by the emotions of speaking publicly about Stella for the first time in all these years, and completing the task with the time capsule, this barrage of memories, past connections and distresses was about to send her headlong into an anxiety attack.

"Oh, c'mon, Freddie. She's not the Princess of Blueridge anymore. Stop gawking at her like you're ready to fall down on one knee and propose," Marcia snapped before she stomped away.

Freddie's cheeks flushed. His face had filled out a little more, the gray eyes she used to think were eerie were now cooler, more reserved. He was still very tall, even taller than Kyle, but still reed-thin.

"It's uh…it's nice to see you again, too, Freddie," she said and this time she did attempt to ease her hand out of his. But Freddie held firmer.

"I was hoping and praying you'd come," he said. "And when Emily announced at the alumni meeting a few weeks ago that you would definitely be here, I couldn't wait to see you." His lips spread slowly into a smile. Freddie's smiles were always awkward and almost looked painful for him. That hadn't changed. "You look lovely," he said and Halle froze.

You look lovely.

That was what the text from Unknown read last night.

"I uh… I gotta go," she started to say and turned to leave. He reached for her again. A part of her knew that he would. But she sidestepped and forced her feet to move faster.

She was walking so fast while trying not to look like she wanted to break out into a run, that she was totally caught off guard when she collided with someone.

"Hey," Kyle said, his hands going to her shoulders to steady her. "Are you okay? What happened?"

Halle looked up at him and let the breath she hadn't realized she'd been holding break free. "Yeah, I…um, no… I need to…um, I just saw Freddie."

Kyle frowned. "Freddie?"

"Rittenhouse," she said and he nodded knowingly.

"And he's still freaking you out." He rubbed his hands up and down her arms now, and Halle tried to focus on steadying her breaths.

Just that quickly she'd gone from standing up to Marcia to trembling in fear just like she'd been last night.

"Listen, I gotta go down to Town Hall to check on something. You wanna walk with me? Get some air?" he asked.

"Yeah, but I need to tell you something." She took a steadying breath. "I don't know if it means anything. I mean, maybe I'm overreacting." But she wasn't sure that was the case. There'd definitely been something strange about the way Freddie was looking at her and the way he'd held her hand so tight. Sure, he'd had a crush on her back in middle school and some parts of high school, until Kyle had not so nicely told him to back off. Even after that he'd continued to watch her from afar and behave weirdly whenever they had to be in close proximity. But that didn't mean he wanted her dead.

Or no, Kyle had said the shooter was aiming at him last night, not her. Would Freddie actually kill Kyle to get to her? The thought seemed preposterous, and yet...

"Okay," Kyle said and let one hand go from her arm down to grasp her hand. He gave it a squeeze and continued, "Okay. Let's walk and talk."

She let him lace his fingers through hers and fell into step beside him. In an instant she felt like all eyes were on them, or maybe just her, and she glanced over her shoulder. Mayor Hodges had said the blessing over the food at the end of the ceremony, so tables were already being called and guests were headed to the buffet line. She didn't see Freddie.

"He said something," she told Kyle. "Freddie.

He said something that sounded familiar and it freaked me out."

"Familiar?" Kyle asked when they were almost across the room. "Like something from back in school?"

"No." She shook her head. "Like something from last night. The text messages."

Kyle stopped. He looked down at her and asked, "What did he say?"

She cleared her throat and prayed she wouldn't sound as foolish as she did in her mind. "He said I looked lovely tonight."

For a moment Kyle only continued to stare at her. Then, as if he were replaying the texts he'd also read in his mind, he nodded and reached into his suit jacket pocket to retrieve his phone.

"Yeah, Bri," he said into the phone after pressing a number on speed dial. "Find Freddie Rittenhouse. Take him down to the station for questioning. I've gotta run over to Town Hall to check on a suspicious package. I'll meet you at the station."

"I don't want to stay here," Halle said even though she knew he wasn't speaking directly to her. "I'm going with you."

Kyle nodded and continued his phone conversation. "Halle's gonna go with me. We'll be at the station shortly."

"Just let me get my coat and purse," she said when he disconnected the call.

He walked back to the table with her and grabbed his jacket off the back of the chair where he'd been sitting.

"Everything okay?" Tamera asked.

"You two hang out here for a while," Kyle said. "Get to know the class, specifically the ones whose names popped up in the witness statements from the murder."

Najee nodded. "On it," he said and stood.

Tamera continued to assess him. "Where are you going?"

"Town Hall," Kyle replied.

Halle slid the strap of her purse onto her shoulder and tried not to let thoughts of the quiet but knowing exchange that had drifted between Tamera and Kyle get to her. It shouldn't be a problem, she reminded herself, if the two of them were involved when they were in Quantico. Even if they were involved now, it didn't matter.

When Kyle reached for her hand again, Halle jumped. Tamera's brow rose as she stared at them.

"Let's go," Kyle said as he let his hand fall away.

She walked in front of him now, heading for the door. Keeping her head down because she didn't want to make eye contact with anyone else. Didn't want to have to smile or talk because suddenly she didn't feel like she knew anyone in this room. Those connections from before seemed so distant now as she seriously considered that someone in this crowd might mean her, or someone she'd once cared about deeply, harm.

"Nobody mentioned Freddie being at the welcome mixer last night," Kyle said once they were outside. When they'd left Town Hall earlier, she'd agreed to walk to the community center instead of letting Kyle get his truck and drive them. Then she'd wanted to enjoy the scenery. Now, she wished the scenery could be the only thing on her mind.

The evening air was chillier than it had been this morning. There had been no new snowfall today and the sidewalks were shoveled and clear. But Blueridge at night looked like a postcard advertising the perfect winter getaway. Tall black iron lampposts lit the way down the row of six blocks that comprised the western half of Main Street. At the center was Town Hall, surrounded by mature trees, with long branches sagging with the weight of the snow.

She pushed her hands into the pockets of her coat and stared straight ahead. A part of her wondering if she would ever feel as safe and for lack of a better word, normal, as she had during the years she'd lived here. No, neither she nor Stella had loved Blueridge the way they'd loved being in the city with their parents. But there was no doubt they'd made friends here, had planted roots that they'd believed one day they could come back to, even if only for visits. Now, in the dark of night, walking along a street that should've held warm memories of great times, she felt stalked. Assaulted. Hunted.

"I didn't see him there," she replied. "Then again, I wasn't really looking for anyone in particular."

"Ouch!" He took a step away from her and playfully clutched a hand to his chest. "You didn't even plan to see me to say hello."

She shrugged. "I figured I might see you. But I didn't plan on what I would do or say in that instance." They passed the bookstore and she glanced longingly at the window of the place where she'd come to purchase romance books at half price on Wednesdays.

"Because you didn't really want to see me." He made it a statement and not a question and she decided she wasn't ready to address that particular subject either way.

"I was worried about coming back here. About what people would say when the surviving half of the Jefferson Twins returned." That was the truth. "I tried really hard not to think about all that I left here in Blueridge. Especially Freddie."

"He was a jerk for the way he continued to bother you," Kyle said. "I pulled him up about it a couple of times, threatened to report him to my dad and have him arrested."

"You also bloodied his nose, so his mother dragged him into the station and told your father she wanted to press charges against you instead," she said. When Stella had come home from the library and told her what happened, Halle had been mortified. There was no doubt that she wanted Freddie to stop staring at her all the time, to stop pretending he was going somewhere else when he walked half a block behind her just about wherever she went alone. But she never wanted any harm to come to Kyle, even if the harm was another blistering talking-to from his father.

"Yeah," he said as they crossed the street. "That was one of the few times my dad actually took my side. I guess it helped that I'd already given him a heads-up about what Freddie was doing."

"You didn't tell your father you were going to beat him up," she said.

Kyle shook his head. "Nah, but I figured it would come down to me getting physical with him, no matter how much I didn't want to because we were so unevenly matched."

"You boxed for the fun of it, while Freddie ran

through calculus equations and trained iguanas as a hobby. Of course the two of you were unevenly matched."

Tires screeched as a car pulled out of a parking spot just as they were approaching the curb.

"Whoa. Whoa!" Kyle yelled and held out a hand to stop it before it came too close to them. When the driver—Mina Carter, a server at the diner and a student at Blueridge High—slammed on her brakes and gave Kyle a wave and sheepish grin, he pointed to the red traffic light.

"Was it just what he said that scared you tonight?" he asked once they were safely on the sidewalk again. "Or did he do something else?"

"He held my hand," she said. "Tightly. I finally managed to pull away, but...this is not how I want to live, Kyle. I don't want to keep second-guessing whether an interaction is normal, or if this is the moment when whoever is after me gets his chance."

"That's not the way I wish for you to live, either."

She sighed because if she wasn't careful, every conversation she had with Kyle could circle right back to them. The long-lost friends. The couple that left a pile of emotions at the feet of their broken relationship.

"I'll be okay," she said with more conviction

than she actually felt. "The Lord brought me through before. I trust Him to do so again."

"You're right," he said. "And this time I'll be there to help you."

"Aren't you supposed to have more backup than me?" she asked—again, not wanting to go there with him. "You told Brian to go back to the station and Tamera and Najee to stay at the event. Didn't you say you had another deputy?"

"Uh-huh, Lonnie. He's on call tonight since I knew Brian and I would be at the event. And, hey, I've got you as my backup."

She cut him a drab look. "Now, you know I'm not a cop."

"No, but you're a pretty smart woman. If we get down here and determine that this package is indeed suspicious, I'm betting you'll be able to help figure out what to do with it."

"Again, you're the cop," she said. "Who's the package from anyway?"

"Don't know," he replied. "Eddie just said it was delivered about fifteen minutes ago and that it was addressed to me."

"Oh, so it's a package for you? Then what makes it suspicious? You're the sheriff so I can see you getting mail," she said.

"The fact that it was delivered to Town Hall and not the station was the first red flag. That, and Eddie says there's too much tape wrapped around the box and my name is in cut-out letters."

"So, what are you, and I, since I'm along for this ride, supposed to do about it? Sounds like they need to call in the hazmat or possibly bomb squad people to open the box and see what's inside," she said.

"Did you forget you're in Blueridge? We don't have people with those special skills on daily staff. Outside of the fire department, for all emergency issues I'm the first point of contact. Then I decide who we bring in if necessary."

Looking over at him, she realized he was serious. "Right. I did forget."

"Besides, it's probably nothing," he said when they turned toward the steps of Town Hall. "Last month there were a few suspicious packages sent to courthouses throughout the state. Law enforcement in each jurisdiction followed protocols to have each package thoroughly checked out. None of them were dangerous, but the governor mandated suspicious package training for all postal and other employees who handled mail. Eddie and his guards at Town Hall, Jolene and everybody down at the post office and my entire office took the training, so he's just being cautious."

"Cautious is always good. Hopefully, you're right and it's nothing dangerous," she said, but when they entered the building and Eddie came jogging over to them, she sensed that wasn't going to be the case.

"You're not gonna believe this, Sheriff. And I'll start by saying I'm not making any of this up. I'm the only one on duty tonight so I'm running all around the building as these alarms are being tripped. I came down there to get you because Lonnie can be a real pain in the butt about things. Especially when he doesn't think they're serious enough to be calling your office. But something weird is happening."

Eddie wheezed as he dragged a hand down the back of his head.

"Okay, take a breath and tell me what's going on here, Eddie. Where's the suspicious package?" Kyle asked.

"That's just it," Eddie said with a confused look on his face. "I left the box right here on this table where I had the delivery guy set it down. After I looked at it for a few minutes and realized it didn't look like our normal mail. Figured it might be loud down at the banquet with the music and talking and all and you might not hear your phone ringing, so I just ran down to the community center to get you. You said you'd be right down, so I came on back. When I got here alarms were blaring. I ran over to the monitors and saw that the door to the artifacts room in the basement had been opened. Had to be without the proper security code since it tripped the alarm."

Eddie was one of those people who spoke with their hands. His hadn't been still since the moment he started to speak. He also seemed to be easily excitable, but she figured if he thought he was dealing with a suspicious package he had a right to be excited, or anxious, which was a better description for what she was witnessing.

"Then I get down to the basement," Eddie continued, "and there's mud and snow all over the floor. And in the artifacts room is where the box that was up here is now sitting. I'm telling you, Sheriff, I don't know what's going on around here tonight!" Eddie huffed after giving that full explanation.

"Turn off the alarm, Eddie," Kyle said, his tone suddenly tight. "Then I want you to lock those front doors and call down to the station. Tell Lonnie I said to grab his crime kit and get down here."

"Crime kit? Right, so we can get fingerprints. Oh my! We've never had a break-in here before, or a burglary," Eddie said, his eyes wide now, voice a little higher than it had been only moments before.

"I know," Kyle said and nodded at Eddie. "Do what I said, Eddie. Now."

Then Kyle turned his attention back to her. "You should probably head on back to the B&B. I can call Tamera to come and pick you up."

"No," she said, the one word coming out in a rush. "I mean, you said I'm a pretty smart woman. And you don't have any other backup right now, so I should definitely stay here with you."

Because she definitely didn't want to be alone in her room at the B&B right now. Not after the weirdness with Freddie and the rawness of her emotions after speaking publicly about her sister.

For an instant he looked like he was going to object. Then he grabbed her hand and said, "Stay right behind me."

Her response was a curt nod, then she walked quickly behind him, the chunky heels of her boots clicking over the marble floors.

"What's happening?" she asked.

"I don't know," he told her. "But if it's what I think it is—" His words halted as he pushed through the door marked Basement: Authorized Personnel Only.

"What do you think it is?" she asked, but a part of her already knew.

Eddie had said the box addressed to Kyle had been moved to the artifacts room. The room where the time capsule was normally stored.

* * *

This wasn't happening. Not in his town and not on his watch.

Figuring out exactly what *this* was, was precisely what Kyle was paid to do. And he was good at his job—he felt confident in that fact. But with Halle standing right beside him, staring at an opened box with their high school yearbook inside, he felt a little unsteady. Not because someone had gone through a lot of trouble to pull out their old yearbook—something he was certain was on Marcia's detailed list of activities this week—but because someone had opened that yearbook and scribbled "criminal" in red marker all over his picture.

Halle gasped.

He dropped her hand and moved so he was standing closer to the box than she was. When he took a step toward the table, she grabbed his arm.

"No!" she yelled. "What about fingerprints?"

The corner of his mouth lifted as he glanced back at her and replied, "I have gloves in the inside pocket of my coat. I was just about to take them out."

"Oh, right," she said with another nod. "You're the sheriff. You know what to do."

And she was afraid. He knew that the moment he'd bumped into her after her interaction with

Freddie. The last thing he wanted was for Halle
to be any further stressed than she already was.
He hated the thought of her in danger and hated
the thought of her worrying about him being in
danger even more.

He dug the gloves out of his coat pocket and
pulled them on. After he lifted the book out of
the box, he flipped a few pages until he came
to the J section.

Halle gasped again and he wanted to punch a
fist through the wall because he hated that tor-
tured sound coming from her. He wasn't surprised by the word *die* that had been written
over her picture in the same red marker. His gut
had told him that was where this was leading.
Their unsub was definitely a former classmate
and someone who'd been close to not just Halle
and Stella, but to him also.

Not that it was a secret that he'd been the bad
boy in Blueridge from middle school up until his
junior year in high school—when things became
serious between him and Halle. She'd made
him want to act right, to be a better person. No
way could he be seen out on dates with her and
have the old ladies from the church, or the guys
who knew his father, looking at her any type of
way because she was with him. So getting into
fights, being suspended from school and as a re-
sult of both, being punished by his father, had to

stop. And as if the moment he'd made that decision was widely known, Ms. Joan had grabbed his hand at the end of one Sunday service and walked him down to the altar for special prayer. His thoughts, his actions, his life, were changed after that. If only he'd known then that it was just the beginning of the changes in store.

"Why?" Halle asked with her voice breaking as she continued to stare down at the yearbook.

"To scare us," he said and closed the book. "He's trying to scare us."

He turned around and knew she was about to continue, but he was prepared to promise her again that he would get to the bottom of this—that he would fix everything so she could go back to her life—when the door slammed shut.

With his lips pursed and the yearbook still in one hand, Kyle stalked over to the door and tried the knob. Locked. He balled his fist and pounded against the access.

"Kyle?"

He turned slowly to see Halle with her arms wrapped tightly around herself. "He's scaring me."

Going to her wasn't optional. Dropping that book back onto the table beside the box and ripping off his gloves was instinctual. Reaching for her and pulling her into his arms was the best thing he'd felt in far too long.

She leaned into him and his mind screamed, "Thank you." She'd been avoiding the topic of them, of their past and what they meant to each other all day and he hated it. Almost as much as he'd hated being away from her these past years.

"Listen to me," he said when she'd laced her arms around his waist and held on tight. He left one arm around her waist, touched the other to the back of her neck, and kissed the top of her head.

"I'm not going to let anything happen to you. I promise you—"

"Don't," she said and pushed out of his grasp. She shook her head and clenched her fingers into fists as she took another step back from him. "Don't make me any more promises. You don't keep them."

Her words, though spoken softly, were like daggers shooting straight through his clothes to slice at him. Dropping his head back, he could do nothing but close his eyes. He'd done this. He'd walked out of her life and planned to stay out of it, but now here they were. It was almost déjà vu of that day on her uncle's porch.

"You're right." It was an admission he was willing to make. "I promised you forever," he said, recalling the first night he'd told her he loved her. "The night of the fall dance. You wore a burnt orange dress." He gave a wry chuckle as he brought his gaze back to hers. "I'd never heard of that color before. But you told me it was your favorite fall color, even found a leaf for reference in that pile your uncle fussed about for days but wouldn't ask any of us to rake. And when I finally just went on and cleaned your front yard, he fussed some more."

She didn't smile at the recollection.

"We danced all night," he continued. "The fast dances and the slow ones. I had such a good time. I always had a good time with you. No matter what we were doing." He dragged a hand down the back of his neck. "I was sixteen and I knew you were the one for me. I knew that I wanted to spend the rest of my life taking care of you, making you happy, loving you."

"And then that changed," she shot back. "It changed and being back here now isn't easy. I'm afraid of whatever is happening with Freddie or whoever is doing this and I just want it all to be over. I don't want any more promises, Kyle. I just want to go home and forget it all."

It was like she had an arsenal of words that could eviscerate him. He was still standing, still breathing, still aching from a teenage broken heart. How was that even possible at his big 'ol age of thirty-two? How could he still be so completely and overwhelmingly in love with this woman, and at the same time couldn't do or say anything right where she was concerned?

He opened his mouth to speak but she held up both hands to stop him.

"No," she said. "I heard every word you said last night. There's no need to go over it again. Just...just get us out of here so I can go."

"I will," he told her and took a chance that she wasn't going to start swinging on him if he approached her again. He wouldn't touch her, even though every inch of him wanted to hold her once more. It gave him just as much comfort as he'd hoped he was giving her. "I didn't walk away because I didn't love you, Halle. I think, sometimes, I loved you too much. So much it scared me. I was supposed to make you my wife, to love, honor and protect you." He shook his head. "But I was an eighteen-year-old with no job. The only reason I didn't have a juvenile record was because my father was the sheriff of the small town I'd walked away from. I had nothing, Halle. I barely had a thousand dollars in my bank account, my mother was gone and my father was so angry that I hadn't immediately applied for the sheriff's department that he didn't even speak to me the morning I left. I had nothing to offer you. Nothing."

She was shaking her head now. So fast and so hard he knew it was to keep the tears he saw welling in her eyes from falling. Tears he'd never wanted to be responsible for putting there.

"You had me, Kyle," she said, the words sounding as broken as his heart felt at this moment. "You had *me*."

"Halle," he whispered and reached out a hand to her.

She didn't take his hand and he wouldn't force her to.

"Stella left me," she continued as a tear slipped down her cheek. "She wouldn't come home with us that night. She just had to keep the party going with Kim and Tasha. When she should've come home with me. We had so much to talk about. How the ceremony went, who wore what, when we were going to finally start packing since neither of us had the time in the weeks leading up to graduation. We…had…so much life to live."

The tears came faster now. Her arms were still at her sides in an almost defiant way now. She wouldn't wipe the tears away, would finally let them flow. He wondered how long she'd been holding all that in. How long she'd refused to let herself voice the emotions she'd tried to bury so deep inside.

"Then you…" She inhaled and squared her shoulders. "You left me, too."

"I'm sorry," he said because there were no other words.

"Sorry?" she whispered.

"I know it's not enough. Nothing I do or say

will ever be enough, but I want you to know that I've never regretted anything as much as I have leaving you." It was a fact that he'd never voiced to anyone. "It might sound cliché to say it hurt me as much as it hurt you, but it's the truth, Halle. I was raised to believe a man takes care of his wife. He provides for her, supports her, cherishes her. My father worked tirelessly to do all those things for my mother.

"And when she died, he felt like he'd failed. I felt like he'd failed, too. He'd failed me a long time ago by choosing work over being at any of my baseball games. Work over helping me with spelling tests or writing papers. I despised him for being so tough on me and for beating into my head all the scriptures about what a man should do and be, when what my mother and I received from him was more physical than emotional. So, how could I expect to be any better with you? How could I do things differently?"

"Leaving wasn't different, Kyle," she shot back. "It was the exact same. Do you remember the night your mother passed and you came to my house? You tossed so many rocks at my bedroom window I thought for sure it would break and Uncle Pete would run out of the house with his baseball bat ready to swing." Her face was covered with tears now, her bottom lip trembling as she spoke. "I came out and sat on the back steps with you. You lay your head in my lap and cried and cried because you said your father had just left you there alone to watch your mother die. You said he'd been at the hospital all day and then suddenly, about half an hour before it happened, he got up and left. And you were the only one in the room when your mother took her last breath. You hated him for leaving, Kyle, and you turned right around and did the exact same thing to me. You left me!"

He sighed but it felt more like he was bleeding, like everything inside that he'd felt for this woman, that he'd felt after his mother's death, then, after his father's, was leaking out of him to leave him empty and raw. "Halle." Her name was a ragged croak. "I'm so, so sorry."

"I needed you," she said. "I needed us." She turned her back to him then and Kyle pressed his fingers to his eyes. After a few seconds he dug into his pocket for his phone. He had to get them out of here, had to get her safely back to the B&B. Had to figure out how he was going to deal with losing her all over again.

He gritted his teeth when he saw he had no signal down here, so he stuffed the phone back into his pocket. He considered going back to the door and attempting to break the lock, but he knew that wasn't possible. The door itself was reinforced steel. The locks were high grade as was the security system. There were also cameras down here in the hallways, if he recalled correctly.

"I'm sorry."

He barely heard the words and spun around to face her. "What?"

She still had her back to him and he heard her sniff. When she turned, she released a heavy sigh as she used a tissue to wipe her face. She must have gotten it from her purse. The small black bag still hung from a strap on her arm, but the top flap was open.

"I shouldn't have dumped all of that on you," she said. "Not now, of all times." Then she huffed. "All of that was in our past. I suspect we've both mourned what could've or should've been for long enough. So, I'm sorry."

She said that last part so matter-of-factly, like this was the only conclusion they could possibly come to, and he wasn't certain he liked that.

"No apology necessary. You can always tell me what you feel, even if it means you're telling me I was a jerk." He forced a smile then and was relieved when she gave him a tentative one in return.

"Well, you were a jerk back then," she said. "Now, from what I've seen recently, you're a pretty good sheriff. I'm sure the town is grateful to have you."

"Oh, I don't know. The sheriff probably

shouldn't have gotten himself and a civilian stuck in a basement." Trying to make light of the situation didn't actually change their circumstances, but he was working on that. "I should've sent you back to the station with Eddie."

"I told you I was staying with you," she said.

He nodded. "That you did."

Then he returned his attention to the wall of shelves. They were filled with file boxes, all labeled. To his right were rows of freestanding shelves. Kyle walked in that direction. He heard the clicking of her boots on the cement floor and knew she was right behind him.

"Where are we going?" she asked after a few steps.

"Well, Brian knew I was coming down here and I suspect Eddie's been to the station and is probably on his way back by now, so it's not like nobody knows where we are. But," he said and finally reached the end of the shelves. There was a space of about six feet between that last shelf and a wall. And just to the right was a door. "I'd like to get one thing right with you." He glanced over his shoulder at her. "I'd like to get you out of here since I was the one who walked you blindly into a situation that could've ended horribly wrong for both of us."

That fact wasn't lost on him. There were so many ways this could've been worse. So many ways he could've potentially put her in danger. But like she'd said, she wanted to stay with him. And he, for more personal reasons than professional, wanted her with him.

He grabbed the handle and yanked on it. Once, twice, then he lifted one foot, planted it on the wall and used that leverage for one more powerful tug on the door. It flew open and he almost lost his footing.

"I've got you," Halle said from behind him.

He had no idea when she'd stepped up so close to him, but her arms went around his waist as she attempted to hold him upright.

"Thanks," he said, looking down at her. She was right there, her face just inches from his and their gazes locked. His heart thumped so loud he thought for sure she could hear it in this solemn space.

"Where does it go?" she asked, her tone a little huskier than it had been before.

"Where does what go?" He found his phone again and switched on the flashlight.

She nodded. "The door? Where does it lead to?"

"Oh, yeah, the door," he said and tried to shake off the mountain of emotions he still had inside for this woman. "The old miners' tunnels are down here. I remember when Spence and his brother Mack and I used to play down by the creek we stumbled across one of the entrances. It was right at the base of the mountain and we went down, got stuck. My dad and a bunch of other men from the town formed a search party. It was a big mess," he said as he led them through the door. "Give me your hand."

She did and he wrapped his fingers around hers. "This must've been before I came to town." She chuckled. "But you were in your fair share of messes after I got here so I can just imagine."

"I wasn't always a law-abiding citizen," he said with his own laugh. "I can own that."

"Do you still remember where to go down here?"

He didn't, but he wasn't about to tell her that. "They're just loops around town and then up to the mountains. But if we find another door close, it'll likely lead to another part of town. I'm guessing there's another one here at Town Hall, since the building is so big."

"What if it takes us to another locked basement?" she asked.

He stopped and turned to glance at her. It was pretty dark down here, but he shined the flashlight from his phone into her face. She frowned.

"Positive vibes only," he said.

"I can do that," she replied.

And when that frown gave way to a shy smile, his chest tightened and filled with love.

ELEVEN

"A distraction?" Halle asked, her brow furrowed. "Locking us in a basement was a distraction?"

Her head throbbed and she was bone tired. These had been the longest two days of her life. One shock after another, fear zigzagging with anger and impatience. She hadn't even given Kyle any argument when he'd ordered her to "sit and drink something" the second they arrived at the sheriff's office.

He'd been right about the tunnel, which had led them to another part of Town Hall—the boiler room at the back of the building, to be exact. That door hadn't been locked and they were able to get up to the lobby just as Lonnie and Tamera were coming through the front doors with Eddie.

For a moment that actually felt like a lifetime, Halle thought they might die in that basement. What if the air supply was short and they eventually suffocated? What if none of Kyle's team were able to get down there and get the door open? Eddie probably had a key, or someone who did could most likely have been called, but she'd genuinely been worried about dying.

Again.

Because having a bullet slam into a man's shoulder less than three feet away was a near-death experience she knew she hadn't signed up for. None of this was what she expected when she'd come back to Blueridge.

"Think about it," Tamera said as she leaned a hip against Lonnie's desk at the front of the room. "If the unsub really wanted you dead—he's already had so many opportunities. You were in your room alone at the B&B for hours today. Now, it may have been a little more difficult to get to Kyle since he was here doing interviews all morning and most of the afternoon, but there was a time when Kyle went home to get cleaned up and changed."

"Two hours," Kyle said. He was sitting on the edge of the desk next to where he'd parked Halle in the chair and shoved a mug of instant cocoa into her hands. "I was at my house for two hours, alone. Then I drove to the B&B to pick you up."

Tamera nodded. "Another prime opportunity to get both of you out of the way if that's what this was really about."

"But this isn't about the two of you, not entirely," Najee said. "Victimology could point to a stalker, someone who was fixated on Stella, but she rebuffed him. Shattered his fantasy of a life together, then he had to eliminate her. Fast-forward to now and you're back in town, doing the thing that Stella would have been doing if she were alive." He had removed his jacket and now pushed his glasses up farther on his nose.

"You're the same complexion, have the same eye, nose and mouth shape. But your eyes are a little darker than hers were, your cheekbones more prominent. She wore her hair long, you obviously—from most of the photos online charting your career... Congratulations on the upcoming tour, by the way. That's gonna be boss and I'm hoping to catch one of the shows." He gave her a thumbs-up. "But you're definitely the grown-up version of what was known as the Jefferson Twins. There's enough resemblance to give life to his fantasy again. You're here, doing the Stella things, so he has to have you."

"He shoots his shot," Kyle said. "And she can't wait to get away from him."

Brian frowned and shook his head. "I can't believe Freddie slipped out of there without me seeing him. I got right up when you called and went looking for him but I couldn't find him.

Marcia said he probably left because she'd joked with him about proposing to Halle."

"Another trigger," Tamera said.

"You checked his house?" Kyle asked Brian.

"Went there as soon as I left the community center. His car wasn't out front and it looked dark inside," Brian replied.

"Head up the mountain first thing in the morning. I saw his name on the list of people who'd been in and out of the resort Friday. He's working there now in the maintenance department," Kyle said. "If he's not there get his personnel file, his schedule. I want to know everything he's been doing in the last fifteen years. Highlight on the last few days."

"But Freddie liked me," she said. "Not that I wanted him to or gave him any encouragement, but he followed me around. Not Stella."

"What if Stella was in the way back then?" Najee asked. "What if Freddie thought by getting her out of the picture, you would be free to be with him? Who else knew about your plans to move to New York?"

"Nobody," she said, shaking her head. "We didn't tell Uncle Pete because he would have just fussed and found some other chores for us to do. He wouldn't have tried to stop us, though. He didn't actually care about us living with him.

As long as he had control of the money, he was good."

"But back to locking us in the basement being a distraction," Kyle interjected. "You don't really want to kill us, but you need us out of your way for a while? Why? What are you doing in the time we're in the basement?" He pushed the sleeve of his suit jacket back and glanced down at his watch. "It's nine-thirty on a Saturday night. Last night you wanted Halle to get the key to the time capsule and when I interrupted her from doing that, you wanted to shoot me, but hit Noel who'd surprised all of us by walking up to Halle instead."

Halle watched as Kyle stood from the desk. He pushed one hand into the front pocket of his slacks, an action that pushed his jacket back to reveal more of the crisp white shirt he wore. He looked professional. And when he began to pace in the area between the desks, she wondered if this was how he looked when he used to investigate cases back then.

"So, tonight, you get up enough nerve to approach her. But why not tell her what you want right then? If you need her to do something, why not ask her while you're in front of her? Why let us leave the building together?" He rubbed a hand over his bearded chin and she couldn't stop staring at him.

"The time capsule is still the key," Tamera said. "It has to be."

Kyle nodded. "I agree."

"So where was the time capsule while we were in the basement? Why couldn't he have just taken it then, if that's what he wanted me to do from the start?" she asked. Fear was still a very real and potent thing, but more importantly, she wanted to know the why. Why Stella? Why her? Why now?

"Spence has it," Kyle said. "When I told him we needed to open it prior to the ceremony, we discussed safekeeping of it until after this situation was resolved."

"So, it's not going back to the artifacts room," Najee said with a nod. "Good thinking."

"And another trigger," Tamera said. "You're taking what he wants at every turn, Kyle. That's why he's going to keep coming for you as well."

"But Freddie wouldn't have known the time capsule wasn't back in the artifacts room yet. Would he?" she asked. "I tried to leave the head table right after the program was over. Mayor Hodges and Principal Gibson were talking so I knew they wouldn't stop me. I thought I was home free until Marcia grabbed me. That's the only reason I wasn't back at the table with you. And it's when Freddie approached me."

"She's right," Brian said. "So, even if Freddie is after the time capsule, if he was talking to Halle, he wouldn't have seen Spence get the time capsule and take it to whatever secret location you and he came up with."

Kyle nodded. "No, he wouldn't have. Besides that, the box had already been delivered to Town Hall—after business hours."

"He sends the box, wants you to see his threat in the yearbook," Tamera added as she folded her arms over her chest. "Who circled back and moved the box from the lobby to the basement? And who locked you in the basement?"

With a serious look that bordered on a scowl, Kyle stopped pacing. "He has a partner."

Halle's fingers tightened around the mug she was holding. "Two people?" she asked and then looked at every law enforcement official in the room. "You're telling me that two people are after me now?"

When none of them answered, she set the mug down and dropped her hands into her lap. Two people were after her and she had no idea why or how they were going to stop them if they couldn't find them. She wanted to get up and run, go far away so that nobody—not these disturbed killers, or Stefan and his Italian dinners, or even Kyle with his conflicting messages—could find her. She wanted to just give it all up, to let go and…what? What was she going to do and how was she going to survive more turmoil?

She knew that rough times were precisely when she should lean into her faith, to let go of the worry and the anxiety so that the Lord could work, but right about now, that seemed easier said than done.

This morning's coffee was far better than the fake cocoa he'd made last night. In his defense, he'd used what was quick and could still be effective. What he held in his hand this morning was an intentionally perfect cup of dark roast with butter pecan creamer in lieu of sugar—courtesy of Ms. Shirley's trip to Lulu's Café on her way to church.

"You don't have to work every Sunday," she said when she'd walked in wearing her pristine white usher's uniform and those shoes that reminded him of ones he'd seen nurses wear in old movies. "There's enough staff to establish a rotation, so that each of you can get your worship time in."

Kyle had accepted the cup and the brown bag with Lulu's double L logo on the front that he knew contained a hot sausage biscuit. They were his favorites from Lulu's and Ms. Shirley knew it, bless her heart.

"Yeah, but since Marcia started that media

ministry, I've been able to join in via the live stream on Facebook," he said as he'd taken the first blissful sip.

When she hadn't left right away, Kyle glanced up at her. "Brian and Tanya need to be in service weekly because they're in counseling. You know their wedding is coming up this summer. And Lonnie, well, Roberta has been trying to get him down the aisle for three years. After their big blowup at Christmas when she threatened to leave him, he's been showing up at her place not only to drive her to church, but also to sit in on the morning service with her. She's about to pick out their invitations and start all that other fluttering around y'all do when marriage is in the vicinity."

He'd grinned but Ms. Shirley had only pursed her lips.

"You're not as cute as you think you are, Kyle Heathcliff Briscoe," she said.

Tilting his head and giving her the smile that had always won him extra minutes of video games when it was past his bedtime, he asked, "You sure 'bout that?"

Her ruby-red lips slowly inched up into a smile. "Well, you are and that's exactly why I don't want to see you closing yourself up in this place, in this work, like your daddy did."

Kyle sucked in a deep breath and released it

slowly. "I'm not Heath Briscoe," he said. It was something he'd practiced saying as a child and for most of his early adult years.

"Yet, you've got yourself all dressed up like him, shined your badge like him, you sit in this office all hours of the day like him, believing you've got to be the one to solve every crime. And at night, you take yourself right back to the house where Heath used to live, sitting at that same dining room table eating by yourself, just like he used to do after your mama passed and you left for the army." With that said, Ms. Shirley had turned herself around and walked out the front door.

Now, about twenty minutes later, he'd finished eating his sausage biscuit, was savoring the last sips of coffee and thinking on—among other things—the truth in her words.

He *was* acting like his father. He didn't even need to contemplate that too long to accept it. But who could blame him? He'd spent the bulk of his childhood rebelling against the man that ran this office and when that man was finally fallen, he'd stepped right into his shoes. Why? Because it was expected of him? Partially, and partially because he'd felt like he'd been training and working in that direction anyway. Hadn't he joined the FBI, become a profiler? Hadn't all of that training set him up to become sheriff of this town? That was what he'd thought, but now with Ms. Shirley's words and Halle's reappearance in his life, Kyle wondered if this job, this life here in this town, was his true purpose.

The sound of the front door opening again, followed by the blast of cold air that swept through the room, brought him out of his thoughts.

The person he saw walking in made his brow rise.

"Good morning, Sheriff."

"Good morning, Aaron," Kyle said and stood. He set his coffee cup down and extended his hand to meet the one Aaron Buckley offered.

"Kyle Briscoe is now the sheriff of Blueridge," Aaron said with a wide grin. "Man, who in the world would've thought this could happen. You got in more trouble than a little bit around these parts."

Not exactly proud of his reputation, but able to accept the truth of what was anyway, Kyle gave a slight smile. "Things change," he said. "Everybody's gotta grow up sometime."

"You're right," Aaron said when they'd released each other's hand.

"Have a seat," Kyle told him, then sat back down himself. "Saw you at the banquet last night but I didn't get a chance to speak to you." And he'd wanted to talk to Aaron, to ask him a few questions about his relationship with Stella and about the night she died.

Aaron unzipped his army-green jacket and removed the skullcap he'd been wearing. "Yeah, man. I saw you sitting over there with your protégé." He grinned again. "Brian was always two steps behind you. I see that didn't change."

"Brian's a good guy," Kyle replied. "He works hard and he's got an eye for details. He does his job well."

"Okay." Aaron nodded. "That means you trained him right."

"I wouldn't say that. He was a deputy under my dad. So, when I got the position, he actually helped me out a lot. Letting me know what was what around here, you know."

"Right, I can see that." Aaron sat back in the chair, let his elbows rest casually on the armrests. "Town looks the exact same but I've seen some new faces since I've been back."

"You got back Friday or yesterday?" Kyle knew the answer. Brian told them that Marcia picked Aaron up from the airport yesterday. But he was interested in whether Aaron would tell him that he'd had another man's wife pick him up.

"Yesterday," Aaron replied. "Had some business to take care of in D.C. so I couldn't get here until then. Sorry I missed the mixer. Then again, I'm not sorry." His thick brows dipped into a frown.

Aaron had been a star basketball player, and he managed good grades or he wouldn't have been allowed on the team. He was a little taller than Kyle, probably around six feet two or three inches tall. While he wore the thick winter jacket and gray cable-knit sweater underneath, he still appeared to be pretty fit. His black hair was low cut and there was a scar on his right cheek, just beneath his eye, that Kyle was certain hadn't been there fifteen years ago.

"Heard there was some drama at the resort," Aaron said. "What's going on, Sheriff? You have a shooter in the wind?"

Everybody in town knew what was going on. Hence the email he'd received first thing this morning from Mayor Hodges. A press conference was set for noon today at the B&B. The mayor wanted to get an official statement out to the town, to assure everyone that they would be safe and this situation would be resolved soon. Kyle wasn't ready to publicly speak about his thoughts on the case. Back at Quantico, they had agents who specialized in dealing with the press, releasing details of a case or profiles, at the discretion of the team leader. Back then that was Supervisory Special Agent Jeremy Sisco, a solid guy with good instincts, who held off on giving those details for as long as he possibly could.

In Blueridge, Kyle was that guy, so he had to decide what he planned to say in the next few hours.

"We'll catch him," was his clipped reply. He wasn't about to sit here and give Aaron details. "So, Marcia picked you up yesterday? Drove all the way up to Morgantown?" Kyle wasn't in the mood to waste time.

Aaron rubbed a hand over his chin. He gave that sly grin Kyle recalled he used whenever he was talking about a girl or getting ready to pull up to a girl. He always thought Aaron presumed it was charming. Kyle thought it was more along the lines of sneaky, then and now.

"You two rekindling an old flame?" he asked Aaron.

Aaron flat-out laughed. "No, sir," he said. "You know how Marcia is, always willing to do whatever for whoever. She offered me a ride and I took it, but there's nothing there."

"Not now," Kyle said. "Because she's a married woman, right?"

"Yeah, everybody in Blueridge is married now, huh? Oh, no, you're not and neither is Halle." Aaron paused but kept his gaze on Kyle. "Now, how did that happen? Everybody thought for sure you two would end up being the next Claire and Cliff Huxtable."

Kyle held his gaze. "I'm a cop, not a doctor."

Aaron gave a wry chuckle. "Nah, you're funny, that's what you are. But it's cool. If you don't want to share how you messed up with her. I get it."

"You wanna share how you messed up with Stella?" Kyle asked.

Aaron's good humor died. "That's in the past. Look, I just wanted to stop by to let you know I'm here if you need any help catching this guy."

"Really?"

"Yeah, you know I went into the service, too. Not the army like you, but the marines," Aaron said, probably trying to goad him into some silly debate over which branch of the military was better, but Kyle didn't bite.

"Oh, yeah, that's right," Kyle said. He did recall Brian saying something about that when they were talking to everyone who'd been at the mixer. "Heard that about you. Served for eight years, right?"

"Twelve," Aaron replied. "Didn't reenlist last year. Got some other plans."

"Okay. Plans are good, I suppose," Kyle said. "Hey, do you happen to remember speaking to Stella at Sharlene's graduation party?"

"You like harping on the past, huh?" Aaron

frowned, then his eyes widened. "Wait, do you think what happened back then is happening again now? To Halle?"

Kyle shrugged. "Just working all my angles."

"Right. Right," Aaron said with another nod. "That's smart. So, the answer to your question is no. That was a long time ago. Stella and I broke up weeks before graduation. And, you know me, I already had my next one in line waiting."

Sneaky and cocky, just two of the reasons Kyle and Aaron were never friends.

"Marcia," Kyle said. "You and Marcia started dating after you broke up with Stella?"

Aaron waved a hand. "That was just a little thing. But you remember when we played that game against the Clovers or Clevers or whatever they were called. The cheerleaders that came and wore those green outfits." His grin widened. "Her name was Tyra, I think, and she was nice."

Kyle didn't bother to ask what *nice* meant. His idea of a nice girl and Aaron's was totally different. Which was why he'd often wondered what Stella had ever seen in this guy. But he'd kept those thoughts to himself at the time.

"So, you and Marcia weren't serious?"

"Never," Aaron replied. "But it was nice of her to pick me up yesterday. And, before you go back into your moral backyard and grab a stick to beat me over the head with, I talked to Rob for a bit last night and he's not feeling any type of way about the ride. The three of us even went down to Gilley's Pub after the banquet and had a drink. Well, *I* had a drink or two." He chuckled again and Kyle only stared at him.

"Are you staying for the full week of festivities?"

Aaron shook his head. "No. I'll be leaving tomorrow. Have some more meetings this week."

"Well," Kyle said, then stood. He wasn't going to get any more information from Aaron and to be honest, he didn't think the guy had any more to tell. Stella had dumped him and he had been angry about that. He'd made several attempts to get her back. Did he kill her because she refused? Kyle doubted it. As he'd said, he had another girl already lined up. And if there was one thing—as sickening as it was then and now—Aaron didn't lie about, it was getting girls.

TWELVE

Kyle needed to see her. To just be near her again before he did anything else. So the moment he arrived at the B&B, he slipped through the front door and immediately found Mr. James.

"Hey, Kyle. How you doing today?" Mr. James asked. The man had greeted him the same way for all the years Kyle had known him. Which had been all of his life, though Kyle probably only recalled the greetings as far back as when he was nine or ten and getting into some type of mischief around town.

"Doing just fine, Mr. James. Just fine," he said. His response to Mr. James had changed and by the way the older man's lips spread into a grin, Kyle figured he was pleased with the adult Kyle response. "Have you seen Halle?"

Mr. James's grin grew wider. "Always knew you were a smart one," he said. "I used to sit out there on that porch and tell Janice that you weren't no hard head like you were out there trying to be. I knew you had the smarts. Natalia and Heath were good people, so I knew their son would be good, too. Don't always happen that way, you know."

Kyle did know. He'd worked dozens of cases where good parents had ended up with evil children through no fault of their own.

"But I knew, especially when I saw you two holding hands one day. I said, 'Yeah, he's a goner.' You know, in a good way. 'Cause I knew that pretty little gal was gonna be good for you. And you for her, too. She brightened up some when you started walking with her and holding her hand."

Kyle felt like his entire world brightened each time he thought about her, heard her name, saw her. He knew why, just like Mr. James knew why he was asking for her.

"She's back there in the café," Mr. James said. "Been back there since she came in from the early service at church this morning."

"Thanks," Kyle said and hurried away before Mr. James could talk to him more.

He heard her before he saw her, and his heart skipped a beat. Just a couple steps before the entryway to the space that had been dubbed the café, where all the B&B guests took their meals, he stopped and just listened.

She was playing the piano. "His Eye Is on the

Sparrow," a hymn Stella had often led the church choir in singing. But Halle was adding a little to it, like maybe it was faster, a little jazzier. Kyle hummed along, the lyrics floating through his mind with her next notes. "For His eye is on the sparrow, and I know He watches me."

In that moment, he was taken back to times when things were easier. When they laughed and played during the summer, sat beside each other during the afternoon fellowship meals on Sundays and went for long walks around the park. It took him back to the days when he felt hopeful, even though he would never have admitted it. They'd all had hope then—it was in the plans they'd made to go to New York after graduation. In all the things they thought their life would be.

Kyle wasn't certain what he hoped for now. He wondered what had happened to his faith and if he was even capable of getting back on the right path again.

But he couldn't dive deeper into that now. The press conference would be starting soon. He'd seen the members from the *Blue Times* when he'd stepped onto the front porch. So he walked into the café and forced his feet to keep going when he saw her sitting at the piano in the far corner of the room.

The sight of her reached out and gripped his heart the same way it had that long-ago day in the church's sanctuary. Her hair was shorter now, her face even lovelier. This was the woman, not the girl he'd fallen so hard for, but she held his heart, too. Standing just a few feet away from the piano now, his gaze locked on her, he knew that as surely as he knew his own name.

"Hi," she said and stopped playing. She offered him a smile when she looked up and Kyle gave her one in return.

"Hi, yourself," he replied. "You're even more amazing than you were at ten years old."

Her smile grew brighter. "Thanks. I miss playing the hymns, though," she told him.

He moved closer until he could take a seat on the bench beside her.

"I do more classical and jazz at the shows I play, so it's kind of what I'm known for now." She let her hands fall into her lap, but she stared down at the keys.

"What about this new concert you'll be doing? Could you add some hymns to that? I mean, if this is your big solo concert, you should have some say in what you play, right? And it's international? How dare you come up in my town and not let me know you're something like a celebrity." He joked because the emotion was growing so thick and hot in his chest, he almost faltered.

"Stop it," she said and gave his arm a nudge with her own. "I'm no celebrity. Just plain 'ol

Halle, the piano girl. Remember Niecey Seaver used to call me that?"

"I remember Niecey asking her parents for a keyboard for Christmas, getting it and not knowing what in the world to do with it because she couldn't be you," he replied.

"Nobody wanted to be me," she replied. "Not even me sometimes. But, to answer your other question, yes, I can add to my playlist. But my manager is always focused on the trends, on making sure we're on brand with my training but still accessible to new listeners. Gospel hymns haven't been high on any of those lists in the past years. Besides, he's currently irritated with me so now would not be the time to bring that up."

"Really? What did you do?" he asked.

"Oh wow." She grinned as she looked at him this time. "It must be something I did."

He shrugged. "I mean, I remember you being just a teensy bit stubborn." He used his fingers to indicate how small and she fake-punched him in the arm this time.

"Not funny," she said. "And it's not really me being stubborn. At least, I don't think so." She sat up straighter, lifted a hand to smooth down her hair, then sighed. "I was supposed to go home today. Had an early flight out of Morgantown. Taxi was scheduled to pick me up at seven this morning."

Kyle had purposely not asked about her travel plans. On Friday and again yesterday, she'd mentioned that she was leaving today. He'd wanted to remain in her company every second he could until that time and figured it could be somehow prolonged if he just didn't ask for details.

To keep things light, he raised his arm and checked his watch. "Uh, I'm pretty sure you're late." It was eleven forty-five, almost time for the press conference, and yet here he was sitting at the piano with her. He thought about telling her that he'd always considered her *his* piano girl, but he refrained.

"No kidding," she said and cleared her throat. "I'm going to stay."

His breath caught.

"Until this is done, I mean. I'm going to stay until you find out who's behind the stuff this weekend and Stella's murder."

He let out another shaky breath but at least this time he wasn't in danger of punching a fist through the wall in frustration or totally embarrassing himself by begging her to stay. For how long, he had no clue.

"I plan to do just that," he said. "But I can't put a timeline on it. Are you sure this is okay? I mean, with your schedule?"

She nodded. "That's why Stefan—he's my manager—was so angry. He's lining up some press stuff, wants to do a photo shoot for the programs. But I can't focus on that right now. Everything Stella and I planned to do in New York is wrapped up in this show. But how can I move forward without knowing, without putting her completely to rest?"

"I don't think you put her to rest, Halle," he said. "I think you keep her with you in here." He reached out, pointed a finger toward her heart. "Stella will always be a part of you, regardless of what we find out in the next few days or weeks. Nobody can ever take her away as long as you keep her in here."

She tilted her head and stared at him like she wanted to say something. Like she needed to say something. Or was that him? There was so much he needed to say.

"Stella will always be in my heart," she said. "And I think, as pointless as it may seem, I think you'll always be in my heart, too, Kyle."

All the words he thought he needed to say fled from his mind. All he could think was now, right at this moment, he could not wait.

When he leaned closer, she didn't back away. If she had, he would've gotten up from that bench and gone out to start the press conference. If she had told him to stop, pushed him away, anything to prevent this from happening, he would've obliged. He would've continued to carry this torch for the only girl or woman he'd ever loved. But she didn't and so he didn't, either.

He touched a hand to her face, rubbed his thumb over her cheek. Their gazes held, hers curious, assessing, acquiescing. Then he leaned in closer until his lips brushed over hers. She went still, but not in fear or repulsion. It was a question he saw in her eyes. The same question he'd been asking himself repeatedly.

Should they?

He didn't wait for the answer, but instead touched his lips to hers again in another featherlight kiss. And another, until his mouth was pressed firmly to hers. She brought a hand up to cup his wrist and he leaned into the kiss. Gave his heart more completely to her.

She'd kissed Kyle.

That hadn't happened in a very long time, except in her dreams. On those nights when she was first in New York and couldn't stop thinking about all that they'd shared. She'd promised herself that during the day she would focus on school, on practicing her craft and becoming everything she had always planned to be. Even if being a musician was only part of her life's plan, at the time. Kyle had decided they would no longer be an item and she'd decided she would find a way to deal with that. Well, for those first few months, she'd done so by making that deal with herself not to think about him during the day. But when she was alone at night, where no one could see her pining after the guy who'd broken her heart, she let her thoughts go free. And they always went to him.

Over the years, she'd had fewer nights where she'd thought about him until she fell asleep. She dated periodically, had dinner with colleagues, with Stefan...mostly with Stefan, who loved to eat. But eventually the sickening pain of losing the relationship she'd thought would lead to marriage and someday children had lessened. Until it was just a dull ache in a chapter of her life she'd tried desperately to turn the page from.

Still, she'd kissed Kyle. About forty-five minutes ago, they'd sat on the bench in the café and kissed. And for most of the press conference, as she'd stood in the back of the room, trying not to be as big a part of what was going on as she knew she was, she'd thought about it. The moment she'd known it would happen. She could've backed away. Could've put her hand on his chest to hold him back. To pause what she didn't believe either of them really understood. But she hadn't.

No, she'd welcomed him into her most protected space once more. She'd let the adult Kyle—the one she was so proud to see in his uniform, leading this town—meet the adult Halle. The part of her that she'd been holding in reserve. Not for him. No, she'd sworn she wouldn't sit on the sidelines, harboring hope that they would someday get back together. She'd been trying to live in the moment, to be present for all things, because tomorrow wasn't promised. She'd learned that lesson the hard way with her parents and then with Stella.

But this was Kyle.

And like she'd told him, he would always have a place in her heart. Now, what she planned to do about that place he held so firmly to, Halle had no idea.

"I don't know if that did any good," Kyle said when he came up behind her. His words effectively yanked her out of her thoughts.

"Huh? Oh, really? Why not?" she asked and folded her arms over her chest.

After church, she'd changed into dark-wash jeans and an oversize lime green sweater. Kyle was dressed in his uniform again and her gaze dipped to the shiny badge on his left breast pocket.

"Because people are always going to believe what they want to believe," he told her. "Especially in a town like Blueridge. Ms. Janice went straight back to the café with Ms. Joan and the leader of their trio, Ms. Gwen. You know they're gonna get their cups of tea and maybe some do-nuts and sit right down and talk about everything they've heard versus everything I just said."

She couldn't help it; she grinned. Then, not-ing the serious look on his face, she put a hand to her lips and mumbled. "Sorry."

He sighed.

"It's just that what you said sparked a mem-ory of happier, funnier times. The three of them always sat at that table closest to the door at af-ternoon fellowship down at the church. They'd have their plates of food, drinks in those dispos-able cups and they'd sit and talk about everybody who walked in or walked out. You know they al-ways had a lot to say about whoever packed up a plate and took it home instead of staying for the afternoon service like they were supposed to."

The corner of his mouth lifted into a half smile. "Yeah, they did."

"And we would grab our plates and go sit in the choir room to eat," she continued. "We'd talk about whoever sang off-key during morning ser-vice. Or who just didn't sing at all." With that, she raised a brow at him.

"What?" He feigned innocence, just like he used to do back then. "I was singing."

"You were not," she countered. "The tenor section always sounded softer when you and Spence didn't sing."

"We'd sung those songs for a hundred hours in rehearsal that Saturday. I don't know why they expected us to get up there and sing them again on Sunday morning," he replied.

"Uh, because that's what rehearsal was for. Duh!"

Now he laughed and she joined him. It felt so good to be standing here with him, talking about the times that made them both laugh. The times that helped them become who they were today.

"I should go back," she said.

Kyle instantly sobered, his eyes widening a bit as he stared at her. "Go back? I thought you said you were going to stay until the investigation was over."

"Oh no, that's not what I meant," she said, then paused because, was that panic or hurt she heard in his tone? "I meant go back to Uncle Pete's." His shoulders visibly relaxed and a slight flutter made its way through her chest.

"I hadn't planned to before because I figured I'd come here and go right back home. Plus, you know Uncle Pete. He's—"

"He's Uncle Pete," Kyle finished for her.

She gave a wan smile. "Exactly. And I just didn't want to deal with that. I sent him birthday and Christmas cards every year that I was gone and he never said a word. Not a card for my birthday, not a call to say thank you or 'Hey, I was just checking on you.' Nothing. Plus, I figured he wouldn't have even known about the reunion. The only people in town he talked to was whoever was at the pub on the five nights out of the week he went there. Like it was his job to sit at the end of that bar and drink as much as old Smitty would serve him."

If she sounded bitter, it couldn't be helped. As Kyle just said, Uncle Pete was Uncle Pete and there was no changing him.

"Everybody ain't meant to be perfect," her uncle used to say. "Some of us got the no-good status when the Lord was giving out jobs."

Neither Halle nor Stella had ever tried to argue that point with him—they'd known it was no use.

"So why do you want to go back now?" Kyle asked.

"Because there might be something there that can help us figure this out," she said. "I was thinking while I listened to you making your statement." In the moments she hadn't been thinking about that kiss. "You and the team keep saying that this is about me and Stella and that time capsule. Well, I remember after Stella got the idea for the time capsule there was a big discussion on what would go into it. She was collecting all types of things to take to the committee's weekly meetings for consideration.

There was so much stuff in our room at the time. And after everything happened, I never cleaned the room. I just packed my clothes and left."

She let her arms fall to her sides, her hands covered by the length of the sleeves. Kyle reached out, fumbled for a couple seconds to push the sweater back so he could lace his fingers with hers.

"That's a good idea," he told her. "If you want to go back, I'll go with you."

The simple act of him holding her hands shouldn't have felt so good. It shouldn't have been as comforting as it was. And she definitely shouldn't have leaned into that specific comfort from him, but she did. "Thanks," she said.

But Kyle shook his head. "You never have to thank me for anything, Halle. You're always going to be in my heart, too."

THIRTEEN

The last house on Maple Creek Lane used to be the prettiest house on Maple Creek Lane. Or at least, the front yard was pretty because she and Stella had read so many books on landscaping and they'd spent so many hours out there trying to bring some life to the place. They'd had no choice but to be proud. Especially since Uncle Pete's only response had been to grunt as he'd stumbled up the walkway one summer's day after they'd completed their design.

On this chilly Sunday in January, the white paint on the old Victorian was chipped in so many locations it looked like they needed to simply hire a helicopter to dump fresh paint over it like they did with water over wildfires. There were several missing balusters to the railing on the front porch, and a chunk of cement had broken off the last front step. The yard was covered with snow today, the bushes that they'd planted to wrap from the front of the porch around to the left side, now a collection of bare branches that she presumed were dead.

"The window's broken," Kyle said and moved in front of her so he could go up the steps first.

The planks of the porch creaked and the wind blew. Even through her coat, she shivered as icy pricks skittered down her spine. Kyle stepped up to the double doors and surveyed the broken pane at the top of one of them. She walked a little farther down the porch to peer into one of the front windows, but the shades had been pulled all the way down. Uncle Pete wasn't a fan of sunlight. For him, any type of bright light was enemy number one to a hangover.

She turned when she heard Kyle say, "It's unlocked."

There was concern in his voice and her heart sped up a bit as she followed him inside. The cold had definitely come through that window into the foyer area. Their feet crunched over the glass on the dusty wood floor.

"Everything looks exactly the same," she said and she noticed the huge mirror on the wall to her left and the console table beneath it. Stacks of unopened mail were in a chipped porcelain bowl on the table. A set of keys was right beside it.

When she attempted to move around Kyle to

go farther into the house, he extended an arm to stop her.

"Stay behind me," he said.

"He's probably down at Gilley's," she countered. "Maybe he walked down because he at least used to have the sense not to drive around town in his condition."

"Probably," he said. "But let's just be careful this time."

She knew he was referring to the incident in the basement at Town Hall. He'd apologized for that when they'd made it back to the station last night, but she'd told him there was no need. She'd insisted on going with him, so she accepted her part in whatever may have happened. But nothing had happened, a fact she thanked the Lord for last night and while she'd sat in church this morning.

They walked through the living room, dining room and into the kitchen that still had the same dingy yellow wallpaper. She ran a hand over one of the cabinets. Touched the spot where the contact paper she and Stella had convinced Uncle Pete to buy so they could freshen up the place, had started to peel. "We taught ourselves how to cook in here," she said wistfully. "Uncle Pete used to fix us microwave meals, boiled eggs or ramen noodles when we first arrived. About a month later, he told us it was a woman's job to cook and since we'd someday be women, we should start early." A dry chuckle escaped and she pushed her hands into the pockets of her coat.

"I remember you telling me how bad it sometimes felt to live with him," Kyle said. "But you also told me how close it kept you and Stella and how much the two of you were learning about resilience and how to take care of yourselves."

"We did learn a lot here." She shrugged. "I guess that is something else we can thank Uncle Pete for. If he hadn't taken us in, we would've gone into foster care and most likely been separated. We never forgot that no matter how rude or unhelpful he could be."

"There's little food in here," Kyle said as he opened and closed the refrigerator.

"He doesn't have anyone here to cook for him now." Funny how she hadn't considered that when she'd packed up and left.

"You want to go upstairs and check your bedroom now?" he asked. "It looks like it's clear down here. But that broken window has me concerned."

"I don't think it's anything to worry about. He might have broken it himself to get in, since his keys are obviously in here," she said and turned to leave the kitchen.

Once again, Kyle took the stairs ahead of

her. He pushed open the partially closed door to Uncle Pete's room at the back of the house. Nobody was in there, just the old queen-size bed and matching dresser set that had always been there. Some shirts and pants tossed onto the floor, boots in a corner, dirty tennis shoes by the closet door. Shades on the windows were pulled down tight as well.

There was a bathroom right outside Uncle Pete's room, another bedroom with bookshelves filled with old books instead of a bed. There were some boxes in there, too, but she didn't pay them much attention. They passed the larger bathroom, the one she and Stella shared, then came to the bedroom at the front of the house. Her and Stella's room.

Halle stopped at the closed door. She put her hand to the knob but didn't turn it. Now her entire body trembled as flashes of her and Stella in this room played like a virtual scrapbook. The first day they'd come here with their suitcases and red-rimmed eyes. Their first Christmas when Uncle Pete had put candy bars in their stockings and gave them each a Cabbage Patch doll. The first day of school when they'd decided to dress alike in light blue denim skirts and pink sparkly shirts with Bratz dolls on the front. Their first Sunday singing in the choir and they dressed in black skirts and white blouses.

The day Stella made the cheerleading squad and modeled her blue-and-white uniform. The Saturday afternoon that Ms. Joan had called to ask Halle to play for church the next morning because Mr. Hannigan, the minister of music, was down with the flu. Senior Prom. College acceptance letter day. The morning of graduation.

"You okay?" Kyle asked and put a hand on her shoulder.

She took a deep breath, trembled, and released it. "Yeah," she said. "Yeah, I'm good."

Just like so many other times in her life, Halle had no choice but to be good. She turned the knob and pushed the door open. Then she stepped inside, expecting more memories to bombard her. But the room was totally empty. "Oh," she gasped. "Oh. Well, I don't... I don't know what to say."

"People grieve in different ways," Kyle said from behind her. "Your uncle didn't cry at Stella's funeral. He hadn't yelled or broken down in any way, from what I can recall. And you said he had no reaction to your announcement that you were going to New York."

"So, his way of grieving is to remain nonchalant? Throw out everything that was in our bedrooms and just forget? Move on like we never existed?" The words burned her throat.

Kyle came around and stood directly in front

of her. He put a finger to her chin and turned her away from the empty space she couldn't seem to stop staring at, until she looked at him.

"People grieve in different ways, Halle," he repeated. "When your mother died, your uncle lost his only sister. Bringing her twin daughters into his home had to be hard because from the pictures I've seen of your mother, you and Stella heavily resembled her. Then Stella is gone and you leave. That's a lot of grief piled into a big ball," he said.

She wanted to see it that way. Wanted, even though it seemed terrible, to believe that her uncle had been suffering all these years, hurting because of the losses he'd endured. And that was the reason he acted the way he did—the reason he was so mean sometimes and so drunk others. What she'd felt all these years, though, was that he simply didn't care enough. Couldn't care enough about her and Stella to do much more than he had.

"Maybe he didn't throw it all out," she said, thinking about the boxes in the other room. "Maybe he just packed it up. When our parents died, Stella and I went into their bedrooms and packed some stuff of theirs so we would always remember."

Kyle nodded as if he understood the direction of her thoughts. "Let's check them out."

There was nothing but old records, blankets and some papers in the boxes in the upstairs bedroom.

"I'll check the basement," she said.

"I'll go down with you, but then I want to go out the back door, take a look around the yard," Kyle replied.

She didn't know what he was thinking now. Her thoughts were too focused on all the emotions being back in this house had evoked. When he left her alone at the front of the basement, she started looking around. There were lots of boxes down here, and the ones on the floor had markings of water damage at the bottom. A stack of boxes in one corner were marked "trash" and she decided not to look inside them. If he marked them trash, then she supposed that was what they were. But there was a trunk a few steps away from those boxes, so she headed toward them.

She tripped on something, yelped and tumbled forward. The "trash" boxes caught her and kept her from landing face-first on the dirty cement floor. But the collision tipped the top box on the tower and it fell to the floor. Pictures spilled out of it.

Dropping to her knees, she scooped up a handful and flipped through them. The winter dance their senior year. Stella wore an emerald green dress that she paid for with part of her earnings from the summer, and Halle wore silver, which she'd selected because it shimmered like snowflakes. A ghost of a smile touched her lips as she reached for more pictures. Cheerleaders, the mountains—they both loved snapping pics of the mountains, especially during the winter when snow blanketed them like a postcard—the church Christmas play and concert. More memories, more time Halle would never get back with her sister.

On a heavy sigh she was about to thrust the pictures back into the box and move on when she saw it. She thought she heard Kyle calling her name, but she didn't answer. Instead, she lifted the paper from between some of the pictures that still lay on the floor. It was an old church program that otherwise wouldn't have interested her, except for the neat handwriting in the margins that was definitely Stella's.

In addition to loving color in her fashion, Stella always wrote with colored pens. Some of her teachers hated it, but flipping through her sister's notebook was always like glancing at a rainbow in print. The words were written in hot pink: Meet me after the ceremony tomorrow? It's important.

The reply was written in a smaller, narrower print and simply read: Fine.

"Hey, are you okay?" Kyle asked. He was out

of breath and when she looked up, she realized he must have run in from outside.

"Oh, yes. I am. Sorry. I just tripped over a box, didn't mean to sound the alarm," she told him.

He nodded and crouched beside her. "Good. What do you have there?"

She dropped her gaze again, her brow furrowed as she read the note once more. "I thought it was just pictures in here, but then I saw this. And I know this is Stella's handwriting. She must have written this note while we were in church since she used the weekly program. What I'm trying to figure out is," she said while opening the program. "Who wrote the response?"

Her words lingered as another picture slipped from inside the program. Kyle caught the picture before it could hit the floor and held it so that both of them could see.

"That's Aaron," she said. "Lifting weights in his garage."

Kyle leaned in closer to stare at the picture, then he reached for the program. "Let me see that," he said and she gave it to him.

She picked up more pictures, saw some random ones of them at school. Fooling around at the park, on the slopes during Christmas break. The heavy sigh that came from Kyle pulled her attention back to him.

"What is it?" she asked.

When his gaze found hers, she stiffened.

"There was blood out back," he said. "It started on the steps, just a few drops in the snow. A path leads around to the side door then there's a bigger spot. There's also tire prints over there," he said.

"No." She gasped and shook her head. "No."

He reached for her then, taking her by the wrists. "We're going to take this entire box of stuff back to the station and I'm going to send Brian and Lonnie out to look for Uncle Pete."

"You don't think—" Her words fell off because she couldn't say the rest. Didn't want to put them out into the universe because then that would mean… It might solidify the fact that she was now totally alone in this world. No family at all.

"We're gonna go back to the station and walk through this slowly," he said, his voice stern. "We'll figure this out. Trust me."

She nodded. "I do," she said. "I trust you." And she did. If Kyle said he was going to figure it out, she believed him. She had to.

They got all the pictures back into the box and Kyle hefted it from the floor. He started toward the stairs and she was right behind him when her phone buzzed from the back pocket of her jeans. She stopped, reached for it. When she swiped her finger over the screen and the text message appeared she screamed, "Nooooo!"

Stella used to say good 'ol Uncle Pete was never worth much but I disagree.

He's gonna get me exactly what I want.

Tonight Baskerville Cabin 8pm. Bring the time capsule or Uncle Pete will be buried right beside your lying sister.

Come alone or you'll be buried with them.

FOURTEEN

Kyle couldn't get Halle to sit or drink anything this time. Instead, she was the one pacing through the office while Najee sat, his fingers flying over one keyboard and then the other. Tamera leaned forward in a chair, elbows on her knees. While he sat behind his desk.

"Okay, here's everything I was able to find on Aaron Buckley after you told me to do a deep dive this morning," Najee started and pressed another key until several windows opened on one of the computer screens.

By the time Kyle had been ready to leave for the B&B, something about his conversation with Aaron was nagging him. First, why had the guy come in to talk to him? They hadn't been close while growing up since Aaron had been more interested in sports and Kyle was interested in anything but the right thing. And even though they'd been dating sisters at the same time, double dates were few and far between. Something he figured the girls had decided, knowing how their boyfriends felt about each other.

"He enlisted in the marines three months after Stella's murder. Was a trained sniper, deployed to two tours in Afghanistan and retired a year and a half ago after surviving an ambush that almost killed him. Since then he'd been actively advocating for veterans' rights." Najee clicked on another screen. "He's been highly visible as an advocate, going before Congress to speak on behalf of the physical and mental health issues facing soldiers after their time in the military. That put him directly on the path to politics, where now there are rumors he may run for congress in Maryland."

"So, we've found our shooter," Tamera said.

"He came to see me this morning to try and get an idea of where we were in the investigation. Offering his help, most likely with the intent of getting closer to the time capsule. Halle didn't take anything out of it last night, only added the new items in. And he'd know by now that it wasn't back in the artifacts room," Kyle said.

A reporter named Margie Franklin who'd come over from Morgantown—since apparently news of their shooter had made it outside Blueridge—had asked if the shooting had any connection to the reunion and the reopening of the time capsule that had been first put away by a former student who'd been killed. He should've known someone else would be smart enough to connect the dots, which was probably why Mayor Hodges wanted him to make a statement. But Kyle had decided he wasn't giving out details and kept that promise, even in answering Margie's question. His response had been a simple, "We're following several leads."

"He fits the profile we had of a stalker, obsessed with Stella and now Halle," Najee added.

"But why Halle?" Tamera asked. "We profiled obsessed because the interest was in Halle from the start, and Stella was in the way. Is that what we still think?"

"No," Halle said. "No. Aaron never liked me, not in that way. He and Stella were the better match. He pursued her and for a while I thought he was really in love with her. He was definitely hurt when they broke up."

"Hurt like brokenhearted, or angry like bruised ego?" Kyle asked. "Because Aaron has a huge ego."

"Okay, then let's revise the profile. Jilted lover, emotional kill. Stella was strangled. That's up close and personal. And it takes a tremendous amount of strength. They meet up, he asks to get back together, she says no. He shouts the clichéd, 'If I can't have you, no one can!' then strangles her."

The sound of Halle sucking in a breath had Kyle looking over to where she had stopped pacing. But she only shook her head. "I'm okay," she told him. "I'm good."

She wasn't, but she was trying to be and he had to admire her for that.

"But she asked for the meeting," Kyle said. "She wrote him that note in church on Sunday and asked him to meet her. Why would she do that if she didn't want to be with him anymore?"

All eyes rested on Halle then, hoping she had an answer.

"I don't know," she said, exasperation clear in her tone. She lifted both hands and ran her fingers through her short hair. "I don't know. All she ever told me about the breakup was that it was time to move on. She didn't want a long-distance relationship with him and she didn't want him following us to New York. She was over him and this town."

Kyle rubbed a finger over his bottom lip. That was the same impression he'd gotten about the relationship. And from the way Aaron had talked this morning, he hadn't been hurt, by any meaning of the word, by them going their separate ways. So what was really going on here?

"The time capsule," Halle said. "The text said for me to bring the time capsule tomorrow."

The moment she said the words, Kyle was up and out of his chair. "You. Are. Not going to that meeting," he said.

She'd folded one arm across her chest and was now rubbing a hand over the front of her neck. "I think I have to," she said, her voice soft.

"I agree," Tamera said.

When Kyle sent her an irritated glare, Tamera stood. "Listen, I know how you feel about her," she said in that blunt way that she had. "I heard it in the way you spoke about her when you first came to us with this case years ago."

"Put him on blast why don't you, Tam," Najee said flippantly.

Tamera shrugged. "Halle's not a stupid woman. She knows how he feels about her and Kyle's one of the smartest men I know. And I know a lot of men, the majority of which aren't smart at all." She moved to stand closer to Halle. "So, I'm sure he's sensing how she feels about him. At any rate, the goal here is to stop a killer. We already ruled out Rittenhouse, since he's been sitting in that cell back there for the last three hours. There's no way he sent that text. And he's got an alibi for where he went last night after leaving the banquet."

She was right about the Freddie part at least.

Kyle sighed. Who was he kidding? Tamera was right about everything she'd just said.

"Buckley is our unsub," Tamera continued. "We need to work out a plan for the safest way to get Halle to that cabin alone, and for us to move in and catch the guy."

"She's right," Najee said.

Halle walked over to him then and placed a hand on his arm. "I trust you, Kyle," she said. "Now I need you to trust me."

"You're not trained for this," he told her. "You have no idea what you're walking into. We don't even know. We profiled the shooter was working with someone else. We haven't figured that part out yet. So, you're walking into a situation with possibly two killers and your wounded uncle. Who's going to protect you, Halle? How are you going to come out of this alive if whatever they seem to want isn't in that time capsule?"

His heart was hammering in his chest, his temples throbbing with every possible thing that could go wrong. He couldn't lose her again. He'd told her that people grieved differently; well, he had no doubt that he wouldn't recover from losing her. She had been the only thing that saved him from losing it completely after his mother's death. Now, with both his parents gone, if she died...

"Hey," she said, cupping his face. "Look at me."

He did and tried not to pour out every feeling he had for her in that moment. The thought of grabbing her hand and running her out to his truck where they could get in and drive far, far away from all this madness occurred to him. Like, he really considered it.

"I'm going to be very careful. I'm going to do exactly what your team tells me to do. And you," she said. "You are going to watch my back. You're going to figure out a way to be right there to step in the minute something goes wrong. I trust you to do that, Kyle. I believe in you."

And now, on top of the fear that just blanketed him so that he was a vulnerable mess in front of his team, she'd made him feel like he had no choice. She was putting her life in his hands, like that wasn't a world of pressure.

"You do exactly what we say," he told her and placed his hands on her shoulders. "Not one deviation, do you hear me, Halle? Not one."

She nodded. "I will," she said. "I will."

There was nothing in the time capsule. Nothing they should want this badly. And yet, they'd kidnapped and done who knows what to Uncle Pete just to get her up here. To get the time capsule in their hands.

Those were Halle's thoughts as she trudged through the snow that was deeper here at the base of the mountain. Nobody lived back here anymore. At least she didn't think they did. John and Susan Baskerville used to have a house in town—a pretty little white colonial with black shutters at every window. They'd raised four children in that house, all of whom had moved away from Blueridge the moment they had the chance. The cabin was for their extended family who, if Halle recalled correctly, had lived in different states along the east coast. John had passed away before Halle graduated, and Susan had been diagnosed with Alzheimer's sometime during Halle's senior year, or something like that. Rumor was that one of her daughters was coming back to Blueridge to pack up the house, put it and the cabin on the market and take her mother back to wherever she lived.

So they would be out here alone, which was precisely what Kyle had been afraid of. Truth be told, she was scared out of her mind, too. She was cold, as the temperature had dropped yet again, in preparation for the new snowfall they'd been predicting. And she was frightened. The time capsule was in a book bag strapped to her back. The earrings she wore were cameras so that Kyle and the team could see everything she did. And there was a microphone in the watch she now wore. Najee may have been the computer techie, but Tamera was the gadget queen.

She'd had a big suitcase full of items in their truck and looked almost gleeful as she'd pulled it out and selected the things she said were perfect for Halle.

"You okay, piano girl?"

Kyle's voice came through the tiny earpiece he'd slipped into her ear just before she got out of the truck.

"So now you're calling me that, too?" she asked, trying to keep a light tone, just as she suspected he was.

"Full disclosure," he replied. "I've always thought of you as *my* piano girl."

Her heart warmed at those words. Not enough to keep her teeth from chattering, but still, she felt all the feels at that seemingly casual admission. "I'm okay," she finally managed to reply.

The snow was getting even deeper, surpassing the boots that she'd had in her suitcase back at the B&B. They came midcalf because she hadn't expected to be walking through the snow. Still, she kept moving. It was dark, but she had a flashlight in hand and she could see lights shining through the windows of the cabin about twenty feet ahead.

"All you need to do is go in and give him the time capsule," Tamera said through the earpiece. "We'll be able to see so we can assess the situation once you're inside."

"What if whatever they want isn't in the time capsule?" she asked. "Do you think they'll kill me on the spot?"

She'd been thinking that question since the moment she decided to come here. But she hadn't wanted to ask it with Kyle standing right beside her. He would've never let her out of his sight if she had.

"You're not dying tonight," Kyle shot back.

And she nodded quickly, as if he could see her. She trusted him. But she also trusted the One who had the ultimate control of how this situation would play out. Her prayer as she continued to walk those last few feet was that His Will be done. In the moments after she'd said those words in her mind, she shivered again. But this time not from the cold, more so from the magnitude of that prayer. She was putting this all in His hands and declaring that she would be okay with whatever the outcome was.

The door swung open before she could kick the snow off her feet, step closer to try the knob or anything else.

"Get in here!" Marcia snapped and yanked her by the arm, practically dragging Halle inside.

"What?" Halle asked the moment the door slammed shut behind her. "Why?"

"Oh, shut up!" Marcia yelled as she stomped past Halle and moved farther into the house.

"Nobody's falling for your innocent routine in here, so you can just stop batting those weird-colored eyes of yours. I swear, you and Stella thought that act was so cute."

Halle followed her, stepping down into the cabin's sunken living room. There was a fire burning as if this were a weekend getaway instead of a kidnapping.

"Where's my uncle?" she asked.

Marcia dropped onto the couch and crossed one leg over the other. "He's back there, probably bleeding to death."

Rage shot through her and before Halle could stop herself, she stalked toward Marcia. But the horrible woman only laughed as she flipped up her sweatshirt and pulled a gun from the waist of her yoga pants. "You don't want to try me tonight, little Halle. I'll do what I should've done before you had a moment to hop yourself on that bus to New York all those years ago."

"Yeah," Aaron said, and Halle whirled around to see him coming out of the room where Marcia said Uncle Pete was. "We should've taken care of all these loose ends back then."

"I don't understand," she said because she really didn't. What had she and Stella done to these two to make them want to kill her?

Aaron looked just like he had years ago, except for that scar beneath his eye and the gun in his hand. He was handsome and athletically built. He might have gone on to become an NBA star if he'd been recruited and received a scholarship. But it was common knowledge throughout town that his parents were financially strapped because of some bad investments his father had made.

"Where's the capsule, Halle?" Aaron asked. He rolled his eyes as if he was bored and she wanted to walk across the room and slap the ridiculous look off his face.

Hurt and anger bubbled inside her but Kyle's voice sounded in her ear. "Stay calm, Halle. We're right here. Just give him the capsule and get out of there."

"I want to see my uncle first," she replied to Aaron. "Then I'll give you what you want."

"Ha!" Marcia tsked. "That drunk."

Aaron chuckled. "He didn't even know I was in the house when he stumbled in last night. He reeked of vodka, just like always. I think he was thankful when I hit him. It was probably the best sleep he's ever had. Bled all over the backseat of my truck, though." He grimaced.

Halle switched her attention back to Marcia. "You followed us down to Town Hall, didn't you?" she asked. "You planned to send that box so it would arrive while we were all at the banquet and you knew that Kyle would go down and inspect it after you just about scared Eddie to death."

"The two of you were always so predictable," Aaron said. "Sitting in church together, walking to school together, studying at the library together. Like two little robots doing all the things you'd see in one of those corny teenage love stories." He laughed but still kept the gun he held aimed at Halle.

"A distraction," Halle said more to herself than to them. "You needed a distraction so you could go to my uncle's house."

"Again," Aaron chided. "Predictable."

"So, she's been your partner all along," Halle continued. "While you were at Uncle Pete's, she was locking Kyle and me in the artifacts room." She gave a wry chuckle. "You didn't really have to go through all that trouble—I hadn't planned on going to see my uncle while I was here. In fact, I should've been gone this morning."

"You weren't going to leave without knowing what was going on," Marcia said. "I could see it in your eyes last night as you were standing up there talking about your dead sister. You want to be the noble one, the shero who finds all the answers and seeks justice for poor little Stella." Now it was Marcia's turn to cackle and despite her having a gun, Halle closed the space between them until she towered over her.

"You will never be as good as she was, not at anything," Halle said. "Even keeping him." The last was said with a toss of her head in Aaron's direction. "He didn't even want you until after Stella dumped him. And from the looks of it, he still wasn't trying to keep you. He left you the same way Stella left him."

Marcia stood and touched the barrel of the gun to Halle's temple. In her ear, Kyle yelled for her to calm down. To stop talking and just hand over the capsule.

Aaron laughed again. "While I always did enjoy a chick fight, I don't have time for this right now. Your uncle's back there. Go see and give me what I asked for," he told Halle.

She didn't want to break the eye contact she held with Marcia, but she did. After a few steps she was at the door of a bedroom. Uncle Pete was lying on the bed, his head still bleeding from where Aaron had hit him.

"Oh, Uncle Pete," she sighed as she went to him and touched two fingers to his neck. He was still breathing.

When she stood from the bed and turned around, Aaron was in the doorway, holding his hand out. She yanked the book bag from her back and tossed it at him. "I'm calling an ambulance to come and get him. You can do whatever you want with that thing."

He let her push past him after he'd caught the capsule, chuckling as she stormed back into the living room. Marcia was still standing, gun still aimed.

"Don't move," Marcia said.

Halle stopped and Aaron walked around her to the coffee table in front of the couch and set the capsule down. Then he aimed his gun and shot the lock off. Halle jumped at the sound and Tamera whispered through the earpiece, "Stay calm. We're moving in."

Aaron opened the capsule and started pulling things out. Tossing Grizzie, the keychain and the papers aside. He flipped through the pictures quickly then cursed. Marcia turned to him. "What?"

"It's not in there!" Aaron yelled. He stood from the couch and got into Halle's face. "Where is it?" he asked. "Where is it?"

Halle shook her head. "I don't know what you're looking for. That's everything that was in the capsule when I opened it last night, and the stuff I put into it. I don't know what you're looking for!" she yelled back.

"The picture!" he replied. "Your stupid sister found a picture of me and I need it back! She was supposed to bring it when we met up after graduation but she didn't have it. She actually gloated about not having it."

When Aaron laughed this time, it was a sick sound. His already dark eyes seemed to go black as he shook his head. "She thought she was so smart, that she was going to hold that picture over my head. But I showed her." He snarled. "I showed her."

"You," Halle said with a gasp. "You killed her."

Marcia, who had been riffling through the things on the table, stood now and screamed profanities. "That's right, he killed her and I happily dragged her limp body from his truck and left it behind the bleachers."

"What?" Halle's chest hurt. Her eyes blurred with tears.

"She tried to blackmail us but we showed her," Marcia ranted. "We got the last laugh. She thought just because she had that picture— 'the only proof' she kept calling it—that she could make us do what she wanted. Well, she was wrong! There was no way I was going to Kyle's stickler of a father to tell him anything."

"Marcia," Aaron said through gritted teeth. He didn't back away from Halle, kept his gaze leveled on hers in a look that she would swear was suffering.

"No, don't *Marcia* me! I'm sick of these two, was sick of them ten minutes after they came to town." Marcia was waving the gun now as she talked. "Your sister thought she was so high and mighty. Thought she was gonna become the next Beyoncé. Took my boyfriend and flaunted him in my face every chance she got. Then, the moment I almost had him back, the one day that we clicked in the music room and found that money, she had to take that away, too."

The music room? Money?

Halle's mind reeled, her body trembled from the force of the emotions soaring through her, then she gasped. The picture she'd found at her uncle's house, the one of Aaron in his basement lifting weights, flashed back into her mind. She'd looked at that picture again just before she'd come up here because it had been in the program. And now she saw it.

"The lockbox," she blurted out. "You were the ones who stole the money from the music department's fundraiser?"

Before either of them could answer, the front door flew open and the next thing Halle heard was "FBI! Drop your weapons!"

"Noooooo!" Marcia screamed and Halle watched as she turned. She seemed to move in slow motion as she held the gun outward and pointed it directly at Kyle, who'd come through the door first. "You and your sister don't win!" Marcia fired her gun.

Kyle fired his.

Marcia hit the floor.

Then Aaron moved behind her, wrapped an arm around Halle's torso and pressed the gun to her temple.

"I'll kill her," he said, his voice deadly soft. "I'll shoot her right here and let you watch her die."

"Drop the gun, Aaron," Kyle said. "Drop it now!"

"Who's the better shot, Kyle?" Aaron asked as he started to move, pulling Halle along with him. "She'll be dead before you pull the trigger."

"Don't do this, Aaron," Najee said. "We can bring you in, talk about what happened back then. Work something out."

Aaron chuckled. "It's too late for that and you know it, profiler," he said. "This was my last chance to keep all this from blowing up in my face. I'll never be able to move forward in my career after this."

He was still moving. Kyle, Najee and Tamera shifting so that their guns were still aimed at him. But Halle knew they wouldn't take the shot. She knew because of the way Aaron had positioned her in front of him. Anywhere they tried to shoot him might hit her. And they would only get that one shot before he killed her. Tears slid down her cheeks as she imagined this was how

Stella felt that night she'd met up with Aaron. In those last moments before he took her life.

"Stop moving!" Kyle yelled. "Just stop!"

Aaron shook his head. "I didn't get a happy-ever-after, Kyle. So why should you?" Aaron moved fast then, pulling Halle so hard against him that her feet lifted from the floor. He was through the swinging door that led to the kitchen and out the back door of the cabin before she knew what was happening.

Cold air blasted against her face as he dragged her some more, until they disappeared through the trees.

FIFTEEN

It was snowing again. Big fat flakes dropped in rapid succession, a glimmer in the darkness of the woods. Aaron held her by her hood now, dragging her and screaming at her in intervals.

"This is your fault!" he yelled. "Yours and Stella's! All the two of you had to do was mind your business and we could've all gone on to live our best lives!"

Halle struggled for the zipper of her jacket. He was choking her as they moved and her eyes watered at the pain at her neck. Her fingers were sweaty and cold so they slipped on the zipper, which felt like it was stuck.

"None of this had to go this way," he continued. "I told her all she had to do was give me the picture. I wasn't going to ask her to be with me again. I would move on, too, and she could go to New York and become a big star like she wanted to. But no, she had to try and be a martyr."

The zipper finally budged and she gasped for

air seconds before he turned, lifted her up and carried her the rest of the way to a huge tree. He circled around to the other side, dropped her to the ground so that her head slammed against the tree trunk. Then he backed away, still pointing the gun at her.

"I told her I couldn't go to the sheriff. I couldn't." His voice broke on that last word and Halle sat up straighter. Her phone was in her pocket so she could try to call Kyle and tell him where they were, but she really didn't know. It was too dark to try to get any sense of direction. Then it occurred to her that she still had Tamera's gadgets on so they could still see and hear everything that was going on, even if it might take them a minute to figure out where they were in the woods. All she had to do was keep Aaron talking. If he was talking, he wasn't shooting her.

"What didn't you want to tell the sheriff?" she asked.

He put both hands to his ears and shook his head. Then he pointed the gun at her again. "Don't ask me that!" he shouted. "Don't you ever ask me that again!"

"Okay," she said hurriedly. "Okay. I'll ask you something else." She swallowed and tried to calm her rapidly beating heart. "Who took the picture in your garage? The one that you thought Stella had put into the time capsule?"

"Marcia," he said. Then he sobbed. He put his palms to his eyes and sobbed. "Marcia was so stupid. She talked too much and she was loud and she didn't think. She never thought about anything but herself." He started pacing again. "All she wanted was to get back at Stella. If not for one thing, then for another. And this time, Stella had won the talent show for the third year straight."

They were sophomores then. There was always a talent show the week before homecoming and each year that Stella entered, she'd won.

"My dad, the no-good, lying, cheating, stealing bum," Aaron continued. "He left us. Just packed his bags and left us with no money in the accounts and my mom just working part-time at the library. Marcia was so angry at Mr. Dunbar. Said because he was the director of the music department that Stella always sucked up to him and he liked it, so he always voted for her to win the talent show. But we were just going to take some of the instruments. I knew a pawn shop over in Cumberland where I could get some fast money."

"You and Marcia stole the fundraiser money," Halle said. "The ten thousand dollars that Kyle had been accused of stealing. But that was the night his mother was in the hospital dying, so he had an alibi. They eventually pinned the robbery on some tourists, but never found the money and eventually lost the case due to lack of evidence."

"If Marcia hadn't taken that stupid picture!" Kyle yelled. He was still crying, the gun still held tightly in his hand. "Then she got it mixed up with some others that she wanted Stella to include in that stupid time capsule. That's how Stella got a hold of it."

But Halle took a chance. She got to her feet and said, "It's not my place to judge you, Aaron." Her throat felt raw; her own tears slipped down her cheeks. "And I don't think Stella was judging you, either. She just wanted you to do the right thing."

"The right thing for who?" he asked. "My family was already the talk of the town after all that my father had done. I wasn't getting any scholarships to college. What was I supposed to do? Go to jail, too?"

Her mind screamed "Yes!" because what did he actually think would happen if he stole from the school? But Halle tried to keep her composure. She needed to buy as much time as she possibly could so that Kyle could find them.

"Stella saw that picture and she figured it out," he said.

Halle nodded. "It was the lockbox," she told

him. "From the music room. We knew it well because we were the ones who put all the grizzly stickers on it." In the picture, the lockbox was on a shelf behind the weight bench Aaron was sitting on. Stella must have seen it, too, and put the pieces together. Halle would never know why her sister hadn't shared any of this with her.

Aaron hit himself in the side of the head with the hand holding the gun. Once and then twice. "Stupid! Stupid!" he said repeatedly.

"I never thought you were stupid," she said and it was the truth. He was arrogant and could be a jerk sometimes, but there'd never been a moment where she considered him stupid.

"I just wanted to help my mother, that's all. I wanted to help her and then get out of this stupid town," he continued. "But Stella knew and she was gonna tell. When I met up with her at Sharlene's party, she told me she was going to the police the next day, so I'd better beat her there. I asked her for the picture again and she said it was in a safe place and walked away. She walked away from me like I was nothing. Like I didn't deserve anything from her!"

And that was when he'd decided to kill her. The realization filled Halle with a heated rage.

"So, I let her go with her little friends. Watched them eating their ice cream. Then they all came out. They walked together for a while and then went their separate ways to go home."

"And that's when you took her," Halle said. "You took her and you strangled her."

"She wouldn't listen!" He raged and stalked over to her, getting in her face again. "If she had just listened! But she didn't so I had to do something. And Marcia was in the truck. She said we had to hide the body, so we left it behind the bleachers. She should've listened!"

"No, Aaron, you shouldn't have been a criminal," Kyle said as he stepped out from behind the tree where Halle stood, his gun aimed directly at Aaron.

Najee came up behind Aaron. And Tamera crossed the snow to stand a few feet away from Aaron's left side. Three guns were aimed at him now.

"Why didn't she just listen?" Aaron asked, the gun still in his hand, but now his hand shook.

Halle moved closer to Kyle, who stood in front of her now. "She loved you, Aaron. At one point, I know that she loved you. But she couldn't lie for you."

"I loved her, too!" Aaron yelled. "So, she shouldn't have left me. And she should've lied for me! My mother lied for my father for years."

"And look where that got her, Aaron," Halle

said. She moved around Kyle then, hurriedly put herself between him and Aaron.

She heard Kyle grumble his disapproval, but she stood there blocking Kyle from shooting Aaron. Sure, Najee and Tamera still held guns on him, but she wanted this chance to get through to him. She needed to get through to him for Stella. Her sister had tried so hard to get Aaron to tell the truth, until she had no choice but to go to the police herself. And for that decision, she'd paid with her life.

Vengeance wasn't Halle's to take. Justice, yes. She definitely wanted to see Aaron and Marcia behind bars for the rest of their lives for all that they'd done, but she didn't want vengeance.

"You know that you're either leaving here in cuffs or in a body bag, Buckley," Kyle said from behind her. "Decide quickly."

There was only a moment's hesitation before Aaron dropped the gun and fell to his knees. "All she had to do was listen," he said and sobbed again.

It had taken Kyle three hours to take Aaron's full statement, handle the paperwork he would need to send to the courthouse first thing tomorrow morning and see Najee and Tamera off.

The recording they had, thanks to the microphone Halle had been wearing, had caught most of the admission, but Kyle still had questions.

"You were on the committee, Aaron. You knew about the time capsule just like Marcia did. When Stella told you she'd put the picture in a safe place, why didn't you or Marcia just look in the time capsule then? Why wait all this time?" he asked when he was alone in the interrogation room with Aaron.

Aaron was sitting with his elbows propped up on the table. He held his head in his hands and stared down at the cool gray tabletop. "I'd gone through Stella's locker. Marcia had searched her bag one day after cheerleading practice. When she set her purse down on the table at the party so she could line dance with Kim, Tasha and Halle, I searched it since she was supposed to give me the picture that night." He shook his head, despair hanging over him like a cloak.

"The time capsule had been sealed the week before graduation," Aaron continued. "They'd already put it in the vault in the artifacts room. There was no way we could get in there. While everybody was at the funeral, Marcia broke into Pete's house. Well, she didn't really have to break in, the guy was always leaving that door open. She didn't find it, but two months after Stella's death, nobody had any leads on who had killed her and we didn't know where else to look for that picture. I wondered briefly if Halle had it but then I thought, no, she was just like her sister. If Halle had known about this, she would've been doing exactly what Stella had."

And that was the truth of the matter, Kyle had thought. Halle would've wanted to tell the truth, just like Stella had. In that moment, he was thankful that Halle hadn't known, even though he was sure she would forever wonder why Stella hadn't told her.

Aaron looked up at him then. "I figured with Stella dead nobody would think about that time capsule again. It was really her brainchild in the first place. But then Marcia called and told me the alumni committee had asked Halle to come back and open the capsule. We were both afraid of what they might find."

"Because you wouldn't be able to become congressman and Marcia would lose the little bit of status she'd been able to build in town without Stella or Halle here as competition," Kyle continued for him.

Aaron dragged his hands down his face and shrugged. "Yeah," was all he said after that.

Kyle owed Tamera and Najee big-time for all their help, even if they both said he didn't. He'd figure out how to repay them anyway.

Najee had called for the ambulance to pick up Pete Coleman, and then headed into the woods to catch up with Aaron and Tamera. Brian and Lonnie went to Rob's house to deliver the news that Marcia had been killed. The town was going to be in an uproar by morning and Halle might be on a plane back to New York.

That was the part that weighed heaviest on him at the moment. It was the only reason he hadn't gone back to his place, showered, got a good night's sleep, then traveled to the B&B to see her at a more respectable hour. What he was feeling right now was urgent, and because time was the one thing he knew for a fact he couldn't get back, he'd thrown all caution to the wind and now stood outside the door of her room.

She opened it, wearing sweatpants and a T-shirt, after the second knock.

"Kyle?" She frowned. "Did something else happen?"

"No. No." He shook his head quickly. "Everybody is where they should be. I even called Vera over at the hospital to check on Uncle Pete before I got here."

"He was stable and sleeping when I left him an hour ago. Well, he was falling asleep after they gave him some pain meds. Before then he gave me an earful about running around in the woods at night and not telling him I was back in town," she said.

"Sounds like Uncle Pete," he said with a slow

grin. "Listen, can I come in? I've got something I need to say to you and I'd rather not have every guest on this floor listening to our conversation."

"Oh, yeah, right." She moved back and opened the door wider so he could enter the room.

Once she closed the door and came back to where he stood, Kyle cleared his throat. "I know this isn't how either of us thought this weekend would go," he started.

"Not. At. All," she replied and leaned a shoulder against the wall.

"You wanna sit down?" he asked, feeling way more nervous than a man his age should just because he was alone with the woman he loved.

She narrowed her gaze at him. "Should I sit down?"

"Uh, no, you can stand. I guess, if that's what you want, that's fine."

"Kyle." She said his name abruptly and with just a little bite to it.

"Huh?"

"Why are you acting like this? Just say what you have to say," she told him.

And she was right. He was being ridiculous. This was Halle. His piano girl.

"I want you to stay," he blurted out. "Wait," he continued when her eyes widened. "I'm not asking you to give up your life and career. I'm just saying that I'd like for us to try this again. To be the couple that we once dreamed of being."

She was blinking, but not speaking. So he continued, "I still love you, Halle. I've never stopped loving you. I did what I thought was best fifteen years ago and I can't take that back, but I can fight for us now. I can tell you that I want nothing more than to try again. I want to get this right with you."

"Kyle," she said and pushed away from the wall. She walked past him, until she stood across the room in front of the window.

"Don't tell me you don't still love me, Halle," he said. "For one, you told me I would always be in your heart. And for two, Tamera already informed you of how smart I am."

She chuckled as she turned back to face him. "Yeah, she did tell me that. And more than once."

"For real?"

"Yup, for real." Halle nodded. "They really care about you, Tamera and Najee. They stopped by the hospital before getting on the road to go home."

"They were my family while I lived in Quantico. I guess they still are," he said.

"I'm glad you have a family," she said. "I'm glad Uncle Pete is still alive with his ornery self. I mentioned rehab when I was at the hospital."

"And what did he say?"

"Well, he didn't curse me out like he used to do whenever the topic came up, so I'm taking that as a good sign." She clasped her hands in front of her. "Kyle, I do still love you. I'm not even going to try to deny that. And for a long time, I wanted nothing more than for you to show up at my apartment and say exactly what you just said."

"But?" He asked the question even though a part of him already knew the answer.

"But not now," she said and looked at him with something that seemed like sorrow. "Now I'm ready to live my life fully. All these years I've been carrying the grief of losing Stella and throwing myself into my work because it was a part of our dream. Now I want to see how it feels to trust the Lord completely and live the life He has for me." She sucked in a breath and released it on a contented sigh. "I want to go on this tour because I've worked hard to get to this point. And I'll dedicate my first performance to Stella and all that she was never able to become. But then I'm going to put all of this behind me. I'm going to keep my sister in my heart just like you said, but I'm going to move on."

"Without me," he said and then held up his hands to halt her next words. "No, I get it. I get exactly what you're saying and it's what you deserve."

Although it hurt beyond belief for him to say that, he loved her enough to respect her wishes. "I only want you to be happy, Halle. And if that means you don't take me up on my suggestion to make Blueridge your home base while you travel for work, I'm okay with that. Well, my heart might say differently," he added with a laugh. "But seriously, I want what's best for you."

He closed the space between them. "But promise me something," he said when he reached out to take both her hands.

"What's that?" she asked.

"Promise me that we'll at least keep in touch this time. I've missed the best friend I ever had," he said.

She smiled at him. "I promise." Then she did something that he couldn't have hoped for—she came up on the tips of her toes and she kissed him this time. "I missed my best friend, too."

EPILOGUE

Three Months Later

Kyle had never been to London.

Yet, here he was, stepping out of an SUV that had been waiting for him outside his hotel half an hour ago. Tucked into the inside pocket of his charcoal gray suit jacket was a ticket and a backstage pass. All courtesy of Stefan, whom Kyle had reached out to a couple of weeks ago. If the man was surprised that Kyle was calling him to ask about Halle, he didn't show it. Instead, there'd been nothing but excitement from Stefan and a willingness to do any and everything he could to get Kyle some private time with Halle.

True to her word, they'd kept in touch after Halle left Blueridge. Kyle had texted her the morning after she'd left:

Good morning.

And she'd immediately replied:

Good morning. I miss Sunny's pancakes already.

He'd smiled and offered to bring her some in New York, even though he knew she would be hitting the road in a matter of weeks. That had been the beginning of their daily text exchanges and while that communication was great, Kyle enjoyed the evening phone calls more. They weren't daily and sometimes not even weekly, but when they happened—when she called him while he was either at the office working the late shift or at home not sitting at the dining room table where his father used to sit, but having his dinner in the living room in front of the TV instead, or when he called her hoping that she'd be finished rehearsing or doing press or whatever else Stefan had planned—his heart was overjoyed.

Hearing her voice, hearing the peace in her tone whenever she spoke of Stella or of Blueridge, the excitement when she talked about what was going on with the tour, and even the surprise when Uncle Pete had called her out of the blue and asked how to make her mother's buttermilk pound cake. Every second of those phone calls was like a balm to his soul. It was like finding the final piece to a puzzle.

That revelation came on the third Sunday in a row that he'd sat in morning worship service. The choir had sung and from his seat in the back of the sanctuary, he'd chimed in on the tenor parts. That gave him a little laugh and he'd almost pulled out his phone to text Halle and tell her that he was singing this time. But he refrained and settled in to listen to the morning's sermon. Somewhere between the time that Rev. Miles read his scripture reference—Romans 12:2—and the time of the benediction, Kyle's heart and mind had synced.

For weeks since Halle had left he'd been struggling with what she'd said to him about not trying to live the life that she and Stella had planned anymore and instead living the life that the Lord had for her. She'd seemed so sure in that statement, and weeks later when she'd sent him a copy of the program for her first show, he noted the addition of not one, but four hymns to her playlist. He'd been not only proud of her in that moment, but also oddly comfortable in the fact that she hadn't agreed to make Blueridge her home again. That she'd been strong enough and sure enough to go and live in the purpose that had been revealed to her.

It had taken him a little longer to figure out his purpose, though. For starters, he had to stop trying to figure it out and just listen.

Halle looked and sounded amazing. As he watched from his seat in the private box to the right of the stage, he was transfixed by her sitting behind the biggest and glossiest black piano he'd ever seen. She wore a white gown that shimmered like satin. Her hair looked even more sleek and styled than the last time he'd seen her. Diamonds glittered at her ears and every once in a while, a brilliant smile flickered across her face.

If his heart hadn't been full of love for this woman when she'd walked back into his town and his life three months ago, it certainly was now.

After the show, he was led backstage where a jovial man wearing a black tuxedo and a bright yellow bow tie stood outside a dressing room door. Kyle knew this was Stefan the moment the man's rust-colored eyes rested on him. It was also obvious when Stefan yelled, "Kyle! I'm so glad you made it," and pulled Kyle into a tight hug.

"Uh, yeah," Kyle said when they finally broke apart. "Thanks again for making this happen. I really appreciate it."

Stefan waved a hand. "And you'll show your appreciation with a nice dinner and an invitation to the wedding. Oh, wait, who am I kidding? I'm gonna be in this wedding, chile. Plus, you know

I've gotta plan it. Have to make sure everything is perfect for my Halle."

Kyle didn't bother to correct the man. She was *his* Halle and always would be. He only hoped that when he walked into this room and said all that he had to say, she would accept it.

But the room was empty when he entered. Across the small space was a table with a huge lighted mirror behind it. A brown couch with dress bags tossed onto it, a rack with dresses hanging right beside it. A half dozen shoeboxes were in one corner and a vase of stunning red roses was on the table. He smiled at the arrangement he'd decided to have delivered at the last minute.

A door to his left opened and she stepped into the room. Her feet were bare and orange-painted toenails peeked from beneath the hem of her long dress as her steps slowed.

"Kyle? What are you doing here?"

"Hello to you, too," he said, totally ignoring the nerves that jumped and crashed in his gut.

"What? Well, oh yeah, hello!" she yelled and closed the space between them to give him a hug.

A hug that was like a breath of life into a man who hadn't known he was walking dead all the years they weren't together. He wrapped his arms around her waist and chuckled to keep from crying. "Hi, Halle," he spoke again, this time burying his face in her neck. "I've missed you so very much."

She pulled away then; the smile she offered was a shy one before she took a step back. "I missed you, too. But I still don't know what you're doing here. You didn't tell me you were coming. I could've gotten you good seats and we could've gone to dinner or gone sightseeing or something. This is my first time in London so I told Stefan I had to see some sights before we head to the next city."

She was rambling and he knew it was because she was nervous. Well, that made two of them. But he went to her, took her hands and led her over to that couch. He pushed the dress bags to the arm and guided her to sit. When he joined her, he took her hands again.

"Is something wrong?" she asked. "Did something else happen?"

He shook his head. "Shhh. Nothing's wrong. I think, for the first time in a very long time, that everything might be just right."

Her forehead furrowed. "I don't understand."

"I love you, Halle." The words just tumbled out. He'd rehearsed what he was going to say during the long flight over here and again in his hotel room, but those words just came without preamble. "I've always loved you and yet I'm just now understanding that loving you was never going to be enough."

"Kyle—" she began but he stopped her.

"Please, let me just get this out. And then if you want to kick me out of here and tell me never to follow you across the world again, I'll oblige." But he certainly prayed she wouldn't say that.

"I told you when you first came back to Blueridge that I didn't have enough to offer you. That I wasn't who you needed me to be. Those things were so much truer than I could've imagined. When I was young, I was trying to be the bad boy. Then I grew up and I was trying to be like my father, to re-create the life he led, just like he'd always wanted. But I had to let those things go, Halle. I had to stop trying to live like everyone else." He looked down at their joined hands and rubbed his thumbs over her smooth skin. "I sang in church last week," he said. "I mean, I joined the choir again and I sang with the tenors."

When he looked up at her again it was to see a sheen of tears in her eyes. But she grinned. "You sang on Sunday morning, or you just sang at rehearsal?"

"Both." He laughed, then continued, "And I put my father's house up for sale."

She gasped. "Oh, Kyle."

"No, it's a good thing. I'm sure now it's the

right thing. I'm not Heath Briscoe," he told her. "I don't know if that means I'm not supposed to be the sheriff of Blueridge anymore, because I love working in law enforcement. So, I've taken a leave of absence. Left Brian in charge and he may end up taking the job permanently, but if that happens, it's meant to be."

"So, wait, you're leaving Blueridge forever? I thought you said you joined the choir?" she asked.

He shrugged. "I don't know about forever. Figured I'd have time to consider all my options while I'm touring the world with my best friend. I want to find out what the Lord has in store for Kyle Briscoe, not what everyone else, including myself, thought I should be."

"I'm proud of you," she whispered as one tear slipped down her cheek.

He released one of her hands and used his thumb to wipe away the tear.

"Not nearly as proud as I am of you." He smiled at her. "The one thing I know for certain now is that I don't want to be without you again, Halle. Not another fifteen years, not fifteen months, not another fifteen seconds."

"Kyle—" she started again, but he leaned in and touched his lips to hers.

"Not one more second, Halle." He kissed her again.

She lifted her hands to cup his face and stared at him for what felt like a thousand years. "Not one more second," she said finally and his heart just about thumped right out of his chest.

* * * * *

Dear Reader,

What a wonderful experience writing this story has been. For my first Love Inspired book, I wasn't sure what this process would feel like. Sure, I've written a lot of stories prior to this one, but there was something about telling Halle and Kyle's story that struck me as a beginning.

Diving into these two emotionally complex characters was interesting because I knew they were about to embark on a spiritual journey that they hadn't anticipated. Both Halle and Kyle thought they'd done all the hard thinking and soul searching throughout the traumatic events that took place in their lives. They felt as if they were now in the place they were intended to be. But the Lord has a way of shaking things up and turning you around until you're right where He needs you to be to do His Will.

I hope you enjoy this story of second chances.

Happy reading,
Lacey